I Hate You
Rock Stars

Brie Kraus

I Hate You
Rock Stars

1

Amanda "Emma" Corzeica has never been very good at hiding.

When she and a group of girls would sneak from boarding school in Connecticut every few months to reach guys at a bonfire, she was always the first to get caught. When everyone has had a rebellious phase and all the girls stole happiness gloss (cherry bomb flavor) ran first when a security guard approached.

Which is why you will understand that her current life on the run makes little sense, as this time it wouldn't be a security guard tracking her, but about 50 SWAT guys; okay maybe that was an exaggeration but not much of one!

The point was, Emma was on the run, and at any second she was expecting the tackle.

"Checking in Miss?" came the polite question from the impossibly pretty girl at the reception desk.

"Yes please. Amanda... uh, Black." No point making it easier for her father to find her.

The girl typed at her keyboard, watching the monitor

before she stopped, her eyes widening. "Um, we were told to expect an Amanda, daughter of the owner?"

"That's me," Emma said without pausing, thank God for Amanda, her friend from her last summer abroad whose father owned the hotel.

"Welcome to The Ritz," cooed the receptionist. "We have you in the Penthouse Suite and if you need anything please let us know Miss Black."

"Thank you." Emma smiled.

Emma didn't have any bags; she'd been in way too much of a hurry getting out of the country to think about that. She'd come to London for three reasons: they spoke English; her father would never expect her to come here because Emma was notorious for despising cold weather; and it was 4000 miles away from where she had been—trapped in New York about to be literally dragged down the aisle at 18.

You'd think that the 21st century meant that arranged marriages had gone the way of corsets and slavery, and died in the 1800s, but no, not in the Corzeica family, not when it meant losing an alliance with someone as powerful as Luke.

Emma walked into the posh penthouse (the size of two luxury, New York apartments put together) with its purple drapery, embroidered with a gold, floral design. The furniture matched the old world charm of the hotel, but possessed the modern gadgets that millionaires could not live without, along with a television in one of the bedrooms tuned into the Disney channel for their children.

The bathroom almost made her cry with joy with its ornate, clawed foot bathtub, which Emma knew would be able to convince her that she never had to run from every-thing she knew and loved, or the fact that 12 hours on a plane had left her hair looking like a giant bird's nest. Just as the warm water started to run, Emma realized that her haste to leave the country meant that she didn't have any-thing with her, not even a change of underwear. The idea of having to get back into her old clothes when she just wanted to curl up in fluffy pajamas made her want to hurl.

Emma decided that a quick trip to a Bloomingdales equivalent was in order; but just as she'd grabbed her keys and shoved her boots back on her phone buzzed.

She looked at the screen, and the words "The Devil calling".

Emma groaned; "What do you want Luke?"

"You seemed to have missed something dear." His icy voice outmatched the turmoil of a blizzard.

"Really, what did I miss?"

"Our Wedding! Did you honestly think you could get away with running?! I've sent men to your house. We will be getting married today."

"Well you're not going to find me at the house, or any-where else for that matter! I will never marry you!"

Emma thought of how she'd rather marry, make out and have sex with the sidewalk than marry Luke.

A stream of aggressive profanities poured from the re-ceiver, so loud that one could hear it from the other side of the room; she pulled the phone away from her ear and hung up. *Shithead.*

That's it; she really needed to get out of the hotel room now. Her hands shook as she shoved her phone in her jeans and headed for the door, slamming it behind her as she turned to lock it, but dropped her keys instead.

"Shit!" Her phone buzzed in her pocket. "Shit!" she repeated, clicking ignore.

"Ahem," a voice cleared next to her.

"What!" Emma whipped around, expecting to be met with the glare of some prude, old lady, but, to her surprise, saw a man, in his mid-twenties with shoulder length, black hair flicking his face as his muscular—and very tanned—arm pushed a door open, about to enter the room next to hers.

Emma's jaw dropped as she recognized his face. He was a rock star; and a damn good one. But that wasn't the reason that he was worshipped all over the world by thirteen-year-olds and stay at home mothers; they loved him because his sexy physique.

He stared at her as though she had just threatened to set him on fire.

"What?" Emma repeated, forgetting to add politeness to her voice.

He smiled at her and took a determined step in her direction when, suddenly, a high pitched tidal wave of screams, followed by 15 girls in t-shirts with his face plastered on them, charged from around the corner.

Emma only had time to say a terrified "Oh my god!" before she was engulfed by the mob of fans and crushed to the ground.

A single thought filled her mind: I hate rock-stars!

2

Emma was sure she was going to die.

She felt like her ears were bleeding with the shrieks that filled the hallway; as she pushed hard against the wall she felt all the air crushed out of her. She struggled, wheezing for breath; two very strong, tiny fists closed around the lapels of her jacket and pulled her up, holding her so that her feet dangled several inches from the red, carpeted floor.

The flushed, freckled face in front of her grinned, displaying the bands on the girl's braces twanging together as she looked a Emma, hyperventilating from her excitement. Her strong, sweet perfume made Emma nauseas.

"It's him! It's him! Oh. My. God. It's him!" the girl wheezed.

Emma feared for her life.

If this was what happened to her, an innocent bystander, Emma feared gravely for what became of—oh shit! She couldn't recall his name. How pathetic was it that she was going to be crushed to death for some famous rock star whose name she didn't even remember.

Just then the freckle-faced girl dropped Emma on her

knees and flung herself back into the mob just as the hotel rushed in from every direction, herding the screaming girls out with pinpoint precision, as though they had done this before.

Emma groaned. Well she survived, but she wasn't sure she would want to if this was a regular occurrence in this hallway. *Stupid rock-stars.*

Emma remained on her hands and knees, catching her breath when two feet clomped across the floor, now littered with hair bands, and even a couple of pairs of underwear, stopped in front of her.

"Are you alright?" asked a deep voice, with a subtle bit of huskiness that made women go weak at the knees.

He should have tried his charms on another as Emma refused to fall for it—she was pissed off! "No, I am not alright!" she screamed, glaring at him. "I was just assaulted by a bunch of shrieking groupies, the likes of which would give a Banshee a run for its money!"

The man chuckled.

"Just be thankful they weren't trying to rip your clothes off."

Emma glared at him. "You're right, I'm lucky they only tried to beat me to death!"

"Here, let me help you up," the man said, with laughter in his voice, as he grabbed the top of her arms and hauled her to her feet. His laughter stopped the moment he and Emma locked eyes and her heart stopped for one beat.

Gray eyes—no, silver—stared into Emma's mundane, brown irises. She had the strangest impulse to reach out and stroke his face, to run her fingers over those high cheekbones and down to his full, and tantalizing, lips. His palms, still rested on her arms caressed her skin just a touch, causing Emma to tingle all over.

The man leaned into her and whispered "Are you a groupie?"

Emma snapped out of her trance. She pulled away from him; her furious steps echoed to the open elevator. "You wish!" she called back over her shoulder.

The man stared after her and smirked: Oh, but he really did wish.

3

Shopping had helped. Emma had bought enough underwear to last her a few months, including one very sexy, little peach bra and panty set that managed to brighten her foul mood.

She indulged in buying almost every decent thing the sales assistant had shoved in her arms until she was well into the 5 digit mark. Emma didn't care; her father had enough money, and was a big enough jerk, that Emma thought he deserved the bill. She thought for a moment about how a couple of days ago she had thought she had the perfect father, caring, generous and kind that he had already set her up with a wonderful, wealthy boy who would treat her right.

She almost cried at how naïve she had been.

She walked back the few blocks to the hotel with only a few of her bags, most of them (and there were a lot!) were being brought over for her when the sky overhead crackled. Emma groaned; England looked more and more like a bad choice for her escape.

Before she had time to think about getting a cab, the

sky opened and rain poured down, soaking Emma in two seconds.

Oh no, she thought. She wore her new peach underwear, which showed through her white t-shirt, thus eradicating her jovial mood.

She sprinted back to the hotel, but it did little to stop her from being drenched by the time she got to her room. Emma sniffled with hot, angry tears as she took out her card to get inside.

She swiped. BEEP!

She swiped again. BEEP!

The card had gotten wet in the storm and refused to work!

Shivering, and dripping water on the floor, Emma sunk down to the carpet about to break into hysterical sobs at any moment. The thought of kicking the door open entered her mind when the one next to hers opened.

Not again, she thought.

But there he was, looking gorgeous, puzzled and dry!

Emma could have killed him.

"Are you alright?" he asked in that deep voice.

"Why do you keep asking me that?" she snapped. "No I am not alright. I am soaked to the bone, about to catch phenomena and now my stupid key won't work!"

Emma felt a little bit like a three year old after her tantrum, but really she couldn't help it. She didn't know how she be even more miserable.

"Want to come inside?"

His words shocked Emma, enough so that she just stared at him. "We can call the front desk from my room and while they sort things out, you can change and put on a fluffy dressing gown." He smiled at her, like he enjoyed himself.

Emma sighed, at any other time and she would have glared at him, but being dry seemed more important. "Okay, but no funny business."

He chuckled as she stalked past him and into his room. It was big, and darker than hers but not quite as nice she noticed. He grabbed her bags from her and pointed to a closed door. "Bathroom's through there, I'll call the front desk while you get dry."

"Um, thank you."

Emma stripped her wet layers off, drying as she went. When she got to her little peach underwear, she let out a quick scream of horror; they were completely ruined!

Emma heard running footsteps and the door was flung open, Her rock star neighbor stood there with wide eyes.

Emma stared back at him, before following his gaze down her almost naked body.

She screamed again.

4

Emma screamed again and flung her arms around herself, but it didn't cover much.

She was—she was beautiful, the man thought as he forgot himself; all he could do was stare at his strange, yet gorgeous, neighbor; at her glistening, olive skin, her hair matted and wavy, and her pouting lips parted in horror as she watched him examine her.

His mouth went dry, and for the first time in a long while he forgot who he was, and that he should not be blushing. His name was Julian Brex, or Jules as most people called him, It's not as though this sort of thing didn't happen to him regularly; he'd seen far too many girls "accidently" turn up in their underwear around him to be phased by it anymore.

So why was he suddenly consumed by a hunger so intense he felt like he might catch fire if he didn't kiss her?

He snapped back to reality when she grabbed her towel off of the floor and draped it over herself with a growl.

"What are you doing?" she hissed, her American accent tantalized him, but there was another accent to her voice that didn't seem to belong: one that made her voice honeyed and exotic.

Jules stared at her, she despite the murderous glare in her eyes. *She must be a really good actress.* "I heard you scream so I came to see what was wrong," he said.

That was true. He had heard a choked off, little scream and figured that maybe she must have slipped, or something.

"Oh…well…turn around!" Her red face exemplified her crankiness, forcing Jules to turn around, an amused smile on his face.

"So why did you scream?" he asked, trying to act like he wasn't aching to turn back around.

"My… eh… clothes are ruined from the rain."

"Oh?" he said, not believing her.

She huffed behind him and he took it as a sign that he could turn back around. She clamped the fluffy, dark blue dressing gown around herself, still glaring at him.

"So what's your name sweetheart?" He gave her his best smile, the one that often made girls fall to his feet. Jules was rewarded by her eyes glazing over for just a second, before they narrowed.

"Sweetheart? I don't think so."

Jules laughed. He was enjoyed this girl, her undisguised fury and disgust of him was, in a weird way, refreshing. "Well if you tell me your name then I won't have to call you sweetheart will I?"

Jules saw her grit her teeth for just a second before answering, "Emma."

"Emma…"

"Uh… Black."

"Nice to meet you Emma uh… Black."

They stared at each other. Jules wondered what color her eyes were up close. From here they looked like a really dark brown, but he couldn't be sure, they were almost—

"Well?" she demanded, sounding irritated.

"Well what?" he asked.

"Aren't you going to tell me who you are?" She frowned at his bad manners.

Jules raised an eyebrow. "Seriously? You don't know who I am?"

"Oh my God could you be more arrogant?"

He laughed and Emma looked at him like he was a pedophile.

"I'm sure this will come as a surprise to someone who thinks they are as wonderful as you obviously do, but except for knowing that you're famous and I'm likely to be mauled by groupies if I go anywhere with you, I really don't know who you are."

Julian frowned, wow that was different. He was, almost, ashamed of himself, for the first time in a very long time.

"I'm Julian Brex, or Jules," he said, holding out his hand.

Emma stared at it, but was saved from touching him when the doorbell sounded and the front desk announced that they had a new key for her. Emma was out the door and into the safety of her own room with only one quick glare at Jules, and an extra firm grip on her dressing gown.

Julian smiled. Everything about her from her glares, to her obvious contempt for him, told Jules that he was unwanted by Emma, making him want her all the more.

5

Emma's chest heaved as she slammed the door behind; her pulse racing, she felt a strange metallic zing in her mouth that she couldn't get rid of. She had to mentally slap herself.

She didn't know why she reacted like this. He had only seen her in her underwear, but the way he had looked at her had been so...personal.

That's it! It was time to nip this in the butt!

Not that Emma didn't enjoy being checked out by sexy, men. She was human after all and no girl in history would have a chance of resisting the smile Julian had sent her, but he was just so arrogant!

The way he had looked at her when she said she didn't know who he was told her that he didn't believe it was possible that someone had no clue as to his identity. Could he be more vain?

Though, not long ago, Emma wouldn't have cared if someone as gorgeous and heart stopping as Julian Brex had flirted with her a few weeks ago. She probably would have already tattooed his name on her arse, but now she knew what it was like; she knew how arrogant, good looking guys treated you and Emma had no intention of repeating her mistakes. So it didn't matter how sexy he was, it didn't matter that his smile made Emma want to rip the clothes off him and run her hands over his—UH!

Emma shook her head, reminding herself that she had to get her mind out of the gutter and back to fixing her already messed up life. She sighed and put on some dry clothes. At least no one knew where she was, that at least was going her way. a sharp, perky knock rattled the door.

God! Did he not get the message that she did not want to see him?

Emma stomped to the door, hoping that Julian heard her furious footsteps and ran back to his room. She yanked it open at the same time hissing, "Julian, I thought you got the message, leave me alo—"

But the insult died in her throat and a frenzied, half strangled sob rose up in its place because standing in front of her was not Julian, the annoying, sexy rock star from next door, but someone else with curly, black hair and stubble, well on its way to being a beard, deep set, brown eyes, with thin lips that curved up into a malicious sneer upon seeing her.

Luke.

He shoved his way into the room before turning with deathly ease.

"Hello, Amanda, or should I say, my wife?"

6

Emma wanted to run and would have bolted out that door and as far away from the hotel as possible if her feet hadn't been frozen to the floor. He looked at her, mocking her shocked expression; one side of his mouth tilted up and Emma was reminded of those Animal Planet shows where the animal grins right before it attacks its prey.

"Don't call me that." she said in a much braver tone than she felt.

"Oh well you're right there I suppose. I can't actually call you my wife, now, can I? You ran away from our wedding," he said, with a smile, but Emma noticed the silent threat behind his words.

"You expected me to stay?" Emma only took a second to push past her fear of him. Who was he to come here and bully her around? Oh, that's right, he was her fiancée.

"Seeing as I proposed to you and you agreed then, yes, I would say I expected you to stick around."

"Well then, Luke, you would be an idiot. Nothing between us was real."

He glared at her. "Oh, it was very real. Just because it

didn't fit your dreams doesn't mean that it wasn't going to happen—isn't going to happen."

Emma glared at him. "I will never marry you."

He laughed so hard that his black curls bounced. "A few days ago you were begging me to marry you."

Emma flushed to her forehead, remembering how she had gone to him and told him how excited she was. How they were going to spend the rest of their lives together, happy and in love. That had been before, before she had learned that she was the only person in that relationship who had thought it was real.

"That was before I found out that you and my father had decided for me a long time ago." Emma's hands curled into fists as she remembered the feeling of betrayal and humiliation. She'd been so sure that he had loved her.

Luke looked frustrated; a wrinkle appeared on his forehead, the same one that Emma had noticed for the first time the day she told him to stay away from her. "I don't see the problem here, Amanda. You love me. We marry."

"No!" Her teeth gritted. "I don't love you! And for the last time, my name is Emma."

He waved his hand like it was of no importance. "Whatever. It really doesn't matter to me whether you love me or not. Tonight we are flying back to New York and then tomorrow we are getting married."

"No," Emma said.

Luke quirked a heavy eyebrow. "This is not a discussion."

"I will never marry you."

Before Emma could even blink Luke was across the room and shoved her hard against the wall. His hands squeezed her shoulders, bruising her skin before he loosened them and stroked her arms. She shuddered.

"Listen carefully, Amanda. I have been very patient with you, but the fact is you have come to be something I want very badly." He ran the tips of his fingers along her chest as he spoke. "And while you are your father's little princess, you know he won't try to stop this marriage. You've run out of excuses."

Emma pushed him away from her and stormed over to the window. Looking down at the bustling, foggy streets of London she felt like crying. She hadn't cried in years, not since her mother's death.

She felt stuck and hopeless. There was no point running again; the bastard had found her in less than a day. There was no point pretending that her father would protect her. Without a good excuse he would never let Emma call of the wedding with Luke. To her father, "I don't love him" was not a good reason.

Emma gave a cranky sigh as she felt arms slide around her waist and another kind of sigh as she was pulled back against a firm chest and a tender kiss was placed on her neck. She spun around. What was Luke playing at, being nice all of a sudden?

But when she turned around it was, "Julian?!"

He just smiled at her, that same smile that had almost turned her into human Jello earlier that day.

Over his wide shoulder Emma saw Luke cross his arms. "And who are you?" he demanded.

Julian turned with Emma still clasped firmly in his arms and smiled at him.

"I'm Jules. Emma's fiancée."

Emma gasped. Rock Star say what?

7

Jules spun Emma around in his arms so it looked like they hugged in a lover's embrace, but all he did was press her face into his chest so that Like couldn't see her look of absolute horror. He knew what she must have thought; and guessed that, in her head, she screamed "WHAT THE FUCK IS WRONG WITH THIS PYSCHO?!"

Jules' own thoughts were not that different.

What was he thinking?! He couldn't just come in and pretend to be some random girl's fiancée, particular a girl who has made it very clear she hates him, not to mention the fact that he did not know her very well.

But he couldn't explain it. One minute he was coming over to her room to—he couldn't explain that either—and the next minute he saw Emma standing there in prime defensive mode while she called some guy, who looked like he's just stepped from the set of a mafia film, an idiot.

Jules had laughed at first. This girl really didn't take crap from anyone and when her stunning little face pouted like that, it did strange things to his stomach. When he heard Luke talk about marrying her and pressed her to the

19

wall, Jules had seen red. Of course, he had not planned to say that he was her fiancée, but when he saw her go to the window she just looked helpless. It was like the tough, spunky Emma fell away and all that was left was a girl that Jules had only met a few hours ago, but knew he had to protect. He knew it.

Suddenly, Emma's little hand touched his cheek and brought his face towards hers. To an outsider, Jules knew that it looked like an intimate gesture, but he knew that it was only so that she could hiss in his ear a second later.

"What the hell do you think you're doing?"

Jules kissed her cheek and whispered back, "Just go along with it."

She looked up at him and Jules' breath caught in his throat. Up close, her eyes went from being a deep brown to a dark blue, so dark they were almost midnight. Lyrics spun around in his head and his fingers itched to find a pen and paper.

Emma sighed and twisted in Jules' arms until she was faced Luke, who irate facial expression burned through the space between them.

"Luke, I'm sorry," she said in an unapologetic tone, "but I do have an excuse for not marrying you: his name is Julian."

8

Luke's eyes narrowed as Jules' arm wrapped around her waist and then ran back up to Emma's face before his eyebrows lifted up. He didn't believe them.

Emma knew he wouldn't; there was no way that she and Julian looked as though they were engaged. Despite he attempts to lean against his muscular body, she found it difficult to pretend to be engaged to someone she had met 12 hours ago, and wanted to murder. Not to mention that she had never been good at lying to Luke, who continued to stand there looking like the anti-Christ about to burn her at the stake.

"Hello." Jules said brightly, "and who are you?"

Luke crossed his arms. "I'm Emma's fiancée, Luke, or should I say, other fiancée."

"Oh, you mean Emma's ex? Emma, love, you didn't tell me that Luke was in London."

Emma stammered. Jules sounded so confident. "I—I didn't know he was."

"Well that would explain it then," Jules smiled.

"You know who I am?" Luke asked, his arms uncrossing.

"Of course. Emma was upset yesterday, after what happened, but she knew that she could count on me to cheer her up. I can't tell you how happy I was when she came all the way to London to see me." Jules looked down at Emma's stunned face and traced her jaw bone with his fingers.

"You came to London to see him?" Luke's mouth thinned.

"Yes," Emma replied. "Why else would I come here? You know I hate the cold." As she said it, Julian pulled her further into his chest as though to warm her, and Luke noticed.

"And how did you know Julian Brex before? He's not exactly someone you forget you're dating."

Emma gritted her teeth. AH! Even Luke, her stone faced, stuck in the last century ex-fiancée was a fan! She heard Julian chuckle into her neck and Emma almost fumed over. "None of your business," she snapped.

"Now, now, dear," Jules said. "What she means to say Luke, is that we met before last year, when I was touring, but—" his face darkened and for a second Emma thought he was actually in pain—"I'm sorry to say, that I left. So we were never really together, at least, not like we wanted to be."

Luke's eyes narrowed even further.

"So you can see why when Emma came back to me, I just couldn't let her go again."

Emma smiled at the glower on Luke's face. *Wow, Julian may be an arrogant arse, but that boy was good*, she thought.

"I see," Luke said. "Emma, are you really going to do this?"

Emma looked at Luke, and the message that she would be his in them, before glancing at Julian; she had no idea why he did this for her, but in that moment, she trusted that he would protect her. "Yes, I'm going to be with Jules."

Luke smiled. "We'll see about that."

9

"What the hell are we going to do?" Emma asked for the third time as she paced up and down her room.

Luke was downstairs, checking in because, of course, he would have to extend his stay to make sure Emma was "properly protected".

Julian laughed from his relaxed position on the couch near the window. "Why do we have to do anything?"

"Be serious!" Emma shot back at him.

She tried to think, and it didn't help that Julian sat there looking like some kind of fiery god, angel man as the light bounced off his hair and made his gray eyes shine. Emma huffed in frustration.

"I am being serious," Jules said with a smile. "It's simple. We keep pretending to be engaged for a while and glary boy downstairs bails back to whatever dumpster he crawled out of."

Emma huffed again. "What part of that is a simple plan? And Luke happened to have crawled out of upper Manhattan, and I fear you underestimate his determination to get me back there, too."

Julian raised an eyebrow. "Are you sure you don't want to go back with him?"

Emma stopped. "As appealing as it is to get away from you, I would sooner lick the sidewalk than go with that A-hole."

"Well then," Jules chuckled. "I really don't see the problem."

"The problem is that you just announced that we are engaged and we haven't even known each other a day. And since we met, I've wanted to decapitate you six times, how could we possibly pretend to like each other enough to get married?"

"I like you." Jules replied with a sly smile.

"You don't know me."

Jules looked at her. He eyed her curvy but slim figure, her tousled brown waves still damp from the rain hanging between her shoulder blades, her high cheekbones and little rounded chin, and her eyes which called him to take her to bed. She'd do just fine.

"I know I like the look of you," Jules retaliated.

Emma stopped pacing again and fixed him with a glare that should be able to kill him.

He smiled. "Just listen, angry boots. You can't have thought that this would have no benefit for me, did you?"

Did she? Emma hadn't thought about what he might be getting out of this; she just presumed he was generous in a freaky kind of way. "How could this possibly help you? I don't imagine your fans are going to rejoice if they hear you're off the market."

He smiled again. "No, but that's exactly what I need."

He paused seeing Emma's confusion. "I need some boundaries. I love my fans, but they are a bit intense."

Emma huffed. "I have the bruises to prove it."

"So for a while, I thought that a girlfriend might dissuade them from me, but, then there was the problem of finding a fake girlfriend who wouldn't end up falling in love with me."

"You really are arrogant."

"Exactly! That's why I need you. You despise me. It fits perfectly," he said, satisfied with his answer.

"Okay." Emma agreed. "So, basically, if we did this, we would be each other's shields?"

Jules nodded.

"There's still one little problem. I'm not a good actor. How exactly am I meant to pretend I love you?"

Jules stood up. "You don't need to fake affection—just passion."

"What do you mean?" Emma asked as he approached her, making her feel like she should take a step back, but she couldn't move.

"I mean this." Jules said, pulling her to his body and his mouth cupped hers.

Julian Brex, the rock-star from next door kissed her and Emma's heart spluttered, before exploding.

Well, she thought, *passion wouldn't be their problem.*

10

From Emma's experience Julian was good at three things: music—there was no denying that, despite his teen-bopper following, he played guitar like Hendrix and sang like a smoky Paulo Nutini; looking better in a pair of jeans than any man had a right to look; and...kissing.

As soon as his lips touched hers Emma felt like she was on fire. It was highly unlikely that she was of course, but Emma would blame the fire for the reason her hands ran up and into his hair, one getting lost in the silky locks, while the other fell down to grab his t-shirt from his shoulder. Whether to push him away, or pull him closer, she wasn't sure.

Jules couldn't deny this was unexpected. He was a seasoned kisser; he knew what he was doing as he had done it many times, but he hadn't intended this. Jules had just wanted to give her a little taste of things to come, just a tease, but as soon as Emma's soft lips parted under his, and she half whimpered, half moaned, Jules couldn't stop. He had to pull her closer, had to kiss her a little bit more, had to...

Emma pushed him away. Jules stumbled backward until he fell, ungracefully, onto the couch. "Okay!" she said, then coughed, trying to clear the gruffness from her voice. "You've made your point."

Jules ran his eyes from her flushed face all the way down to her knotted hands. "Oh, I haven't even started making my point." He stepped towards her. "Why don't I finish?"

"No!" Emma held up her hands like a shield. "I am not a play toy. If you can't reign in your libido then go get your frisk on with one of the 20 groupies camped outside the hotel."

Jules smiled. "I can't, remember. I'm off the market."

Emma glared at him. "Sorry honey, I forgot."

He chuckled.

"From now on let's just keep the touching to what is strictly necessary."

"Whatever you desire, my dear." Jules quirked an eyebrow and Emma shot up in flames all over again when his voice slowed on the word desire.

There was a moment of silence as Jules looked at her with those laughing eyes and Emma contemplated punching him to make him stop.

"You should go get changed," he said.

"Why?" Emma placed her hands to her hips.

"Because I'm hungry and have a very good reason for going out. Publicity."

Emma cringed. She didn't like photos; for some reason her face always ended up looking puckered and squinty. But she knew that she owed Julian this, and was relieved that he got something out of it. Not that she expected his plan to work—those groupies from the hall earlier were not lightweights. It would take more than a skinny, little American to ward them off of getting their hands on a piece of Julian meat.

With a huff, Emma stormed off to her room and emerged 15 minutes later with dry hair, mascara, and a little blue dress which managed to say "I'm not trying too hard, but still, I'm gorgeous."

Julian's eyes roamed up and down her body from his lazy position on the couch, ending with another one of those smiles which made Emma's heart falter for a second, but only a second. To her dismay, she noticed that the only alternation he'd made to his wardrobe was a beaten up leather jacket.

Emma glared at him. "So you don't have to change?"

"Why would I? I always look good."

"AH!" Emma shrieked, disgusted, before turning and stomping out the door.

Emma heard him laugh as he jogged to catch up to her, tangling his hand with hers when he got there. She stopped mid stride and glared at their locked hands. "What do you think you're doing?" she demanded.

"Holding hands with my fiancée." Jules leant in closer to whisper, "We're supposed to be in love remember?"

Emma's thoughts blurred for a second. He smelled wonderful: peppermint and that odor that precedes thunderstorm. She mentally slapped herself again. "Yes I remember, but while no one's going to see, us we should be on a strictly no contact terms. When we get to the lobby, you can hold my hand."

Jules released her hand. "Can't wait."

Emma groaned. This was going to be the longest fake engagement ever.

11

The elevator ride dragged, causing Emma's hand to tingle with each passing second. She needed to be able to think right now; she needed to be able to figure out how she was going to pull this off. Obviously, she wasn't going to marry Luke, and the thought of marrying Julian made her face pucker the way lemons did. Emma just needed a little time, just a while to convince Luke that he didn't have a chance with her, so that he would leave and forget about their engagement, but she couldn't afford focus on any of these things—couldn't focus on her very important, very tragic upcoming future because she still tingled from Julian. Emma glared at him. He smiled to himself the entire way down; his full lips pulled back in a way that said he was very pleased with himself.

Damn him!

As soon as the doors slid open Julian locked his fingers with hers. "I'm so glad we're back together."

Emma resisted the urge to break his fingers under hers. Instead, she just gave Julian an amazing ear to ear grin, and while it was clearly the most sarcastic thing in history, just seeing her smile made Julian's witty response die in his throat.

She smiled again, this time with victory, and tugged him towards the revolving doors. They both jerked to a halt when a dark voice whipped across the lobby.

"Amanda!"

Emma sighed and she heard Julian chuckle "Amanda" at her back.

"Luke," she replied, plastering on another fake smile, "I thought you would have left by now. At least, I hoped you would have."

Luke raised a dark eyebrow. "No such luck," he said, in a jovial tone.

"Well, we'd love to stay and chat, but, actually, Julian and I have a dinner to get to, and I might puke if I stay around you much longer."

With that and a glare Emma pulled Julian away. "Come on, babe, I can't wait to get you alone," she seductively whispered into Jules' ear, but loud enough for Luke to over-hear. Emma almost heard his jaw snap shut behind them.

Jules leant down and grazed his lips against her earlobe. "I can't wait either," he whispered.

Emma gulped, but was interrupted again by Luke.

"Oh and Amanda, I've managed to check in just down the hall from you. That way I'll be able to show your father around when he gets here."

Emma stopped. "Father's coming?"

Luke smiled. "He leaves New York tomorrow. He can't wait to meet your…fiancée."

Okay, Emma thought, *this night was not going well.*

She had been so dazed by Luke mentioning that her father was coming to London, that she hadn't been prepared when she burst through the revolving doors of the Ritz hand in hand with Julian, only to be met by 20 photographers and a whole slew of screaming fans.

It was insanity, as though they all thought they were dying, and a picture of Julian would save them. She wanted to call them crazy and desperate, but she couldn't blame them for thinking he was something worth worshipping. On the outside, he was practically a god, if only the inside was a little more shiny.

Though Emma did not understand their fascination for the rock star, she still couldn't figure out why in the hell they looked like they wanted a piece of her! Her vision blurred from all of the camera flashes which had gone off right in her face, and she could have sworn she heard someone describing every detail of her outfit into a little portable recorder, telling her that she would have to dress with more care.

20 minutes later Julian had elbowed his way through the crowd, smiling and waving the entire time, to a waiting car in which they had spent a silent ride with Emma's head between her knees trying to stop the dizziness. They arrived at a small, smoky restaurant tucked away from all of the bustle of London. Emma let out a heavy sigh of relief as Julian guided her to a dark booth and ordered her a comforting hot chocolate.

"That was—is it always like that?" she asked, looking up to see his gray eyes laughing.

"Pretty much," he said. "What can I say? I'm a pretty popular guy."

Emma slapped her forehead with her palm. She would never feel sorry for him again.

"No wonder you couldn't get someone to be your girlfriend before. When you're not being totally conceited, then your date is getting mauled outside of every doorway."

"Not every doorway."

Emma's eyes narrowed. "You are infuriating."

"You're cute when you're angry. Lucky for me, considering you're, pretty much, always angry." Jules smirked at her, a bit of the devil in his grin.

Emma rolled her eyes. "Why should I be cheery? In case you haven't noticed, I've been forced into two engagements, fled the country, and been assaulted by your groupies twice in the last 24 hours."

This did warrant her a serious look from Julian for once. "About that, I think you should tell me exactly what's going on with you and Luke?"

12

Emma looked away. "There's not much to tell."

"I'll be the judge of that." Julian replied. "For some reason, I find it hard to believe that an engagement isn't much to tell."

Emma's face tightened. "It wasn't a real engagement."

"Luke seems to think it was."

"Luke's an asshole."

Jules chuckled. "Yeah, I kind of gathered that, but I still don't understand why you needed someone to pretend to be your fiancée so you could get out of marrying him?"

Emma sighed and Jules moved closer to her in the booth.

"Growing up I spent half my time between Maine and New York and I—I guess we were always wealthy. I never really thought about it, I just knew that I went to good schools and had nice things, I never thought about where they came from, but when I was 16 I went to spend my summer in New York, and my father introduced me to Luke." She grimaced at Jules, almost apologetically.

"I had a huge crush on him the moment I saw him. He was so confident and sure of himself, and so sure of me. He knew that I would like him. But I always stayed away; he was four years older than me and really he—he scared me a little, but I thought that was just because I liked him so much, and because his family was so rich. Really, they made my family seem like paupers; it was ridiculous. Anyway, after that summer, we went back to Maine and…my mom died."

She stopped speaking and Jules wiped a tear away that she hadn't known she'd let loose. Emma hadn't spoken about any of this in so long, and she still hadn't told any of her friends about finding out about Luke.

"I didn't know then, but after mom died, my dad went on a kind of spending spree. He didn't tell me, but we were in debt, to Luke's family. So when Luke came to me and said he wanted us to be together, and, then, a few weeks later that he wanted us to get married, I didn't know it was because I was the repayment for the debt my dad had acquired. I thought he loved me. I was stupid, I was infatuated with him, but it was all a lie.

"The wedding was booked for a week after I turned 18. I found that out yesterday—three days before the wedding, and I ran." Emma gave Jules a mocking smile. "And now I'm here."

Jules frowned, remaining quiet for a while, thinking about what she had confided in him, and Emma wondered whether he reconsidered getting involved.

"Okay," he said, finally, "he really is an asshole, but I don't understand, as lovely as you are, why would Luke's family accept you as payment?"

Emma laughed. "Oh, it wasn't me they wanted. My grandfather was another member of my family who was stuck in the middle ages; he thought that a girl should marry as soon as possible, so he left me an inheritance—collectable as soon as I'm a bride. The clock starts counting down as soon as I turn 18, and every year that I wait to get married the money goes down."

Julian's eyebrows raised. "Geez, your family is very dramatic, isn't it?"

"You have no idea."

"How much is the inheritance?" Jules asked, while taking a sip from his beer.

"20 million dollars."

Beer spurted from Jules' nose. "20 million!"

"Yep. Going down a million every year I wait."

Jules shook his head, "Well, Jesus, no wonder Luke wanted to marry you."

The moment the words had blurted from his mouth, Emma's eyes welled up with angry tears and Julian was worried for a second that she would hit him. Instead, she just said, "Exactly, so now you can see why I had to leave."

"Sure," he replied.

Dinner had left Emma rattled. Why did she tell him all of that? Why did he listen?

In a way Emma had to admit that if felt good to let it all out, even if she was letting it out to Julian. Emma had been surprised when he hadn't laughed at her, or made some cheesy joke, like she had expected him to.

They went through the doors to the Ritz with the same frenzy of groupies, and the press, almost beating them to death before they made it inside, and up to their rooms. Julian stopped outside of her door as though they were on a real date, but Emma avoided looking at him.

13

It didn't matter how good of a listener Julian had been tonight, she still thought he was one of the most conceited people she had ever met, and she'd had quite enough of confident, lying boys to last her a lifetime.

"Emma," he said, when she opened the door, "I'm sorry about what happened to you and Luke."

"Thanks," she replied, saddened again as she remembered.

"But you'll get over it soon."

Emma's head snapped up. He was smirking. "Why's that?" she demanded.

"Because you didn't love him."

"What?! Yes I—"

"No you didn't." Jules interrupted her, "I bet you didn't even want him."

Emma was livid. She let the door swing shut as she came close to him and put her hands on her hips.

He smiled. "Not like you want me."

Emma raised her fist to punch him, but Julian was quicker, and before she could react, she was in his arms and Julian kissed her, again. *This was getting to be a bad habit,*

Emma thought. She couldn't keep letting Julian prove his point with kisses that numbed her brain and made it impossible to think straight. If she was thinking clearly, she would never be doing what she was doing now, wrapping her arms around Julian's neck and pulling herself up, deepening kiss. She would never have moaned and arched into him as he pushed her against the wall and pressed his humming body into hers; and she most certainly wouldn't have felt as though he electrocuted her with constant jolts of pleasure that zipped up and down her veins like fire.

Emma wanted him. She had to admit that to herself. The way her body reacted was proof that what he had said was true.

She had wanted Luke too, but in such a different way. With Luke, she loved to feel his lips on hers and his hands roaming her body because it meant that he wanted her. That he desired her.

Her need for Julian was different. He desired her. Emma felt that longing in his hot and heavy kiss. She wanted him to touch her, to caress her, and because he made her feel more alive than she thought was possible, pushed even deeper into his body.

The small part of her brain that still managed to function, despite their fevered passion, reasoned that admitting she was attracted to Julian wasn't bad; he was an international superstar, not to mention the sexiest man she's ever seen—there was no harm in a few kisses…

Jules pulled his mouth from hers and buried it in her neck, overcome with his own longing, and murmured, "Emma" into her soft skin.

That was all she needed, just that one little wakeup call of his voice to jolt her out of her kissing coma.

Emma pulled back, her arms around his neck loosened and pushed him from her. She looked at him for one second, his gray eyes burning and his arms looking empty as she recalled her own fast breathing and rumpled dress. She pushed her door open and slammed it behind her.

Oh god, she thought, *I'm a freaking groupie*!

14

Alright, Jules thought, *time for a cold shower*.

He didn't know why he kept doing this to himself. Why he kept kissing Emma when he knew that it had to end. He should know by now that she was just going to push him away, not because she didn't want him—she had proven that she desired him when she gasped and lengthened the kiss. No, Emma pushed him away because she was scared, and more than a little hostile. He couldn't blame her; Luke had damaged her emotionally when he used her like that.

Jules related. He couldn't count the amount of girls (and some boys) who had tried to be with him for his money, or fame, for the people he knew, or the lifestyle he could give them. He supposed the only difference between him and Emma was that Jules always knew that they were gold-digging bitches, whereas Emma had really thought Luke loved her. That guy deserved a good thrashing and Jules hoped for the chance to give him one. The thought of it made him smile, but Emma was so feisty she'd probably beat him to it, and whoop his ass herself.

She was…unusual. Beautiful, there was no doubt about

that, but Jules thought that he just wouldn't be able to impress her. Maybe she actually didn't want him. He laughed. *Yeah, sure she didn't, Julian.*

He, himself, wasn't sure what he wanted from her. He didn't date, so it wasn't that, and it wasn't because he needed someone to sleep with. He could pick someone off the street who was more than willing to meet his needs, and he knew that. Maybe it was that Julian hadn't had a challenge in a long time, not since his songs made the air and the small production company he was partner in started signing great artists.

That must be it then, he thought to himself, *the challenge. It must be that challenge. I mean, what else could it be?*

While Julian debated with himself over why he desired this American girl, Emma tossed and turned, unable to sleep. She would fall into dreams, at first, languid and charming, like being asleep in a sunny meadow, and then, suddenly, hands touched her body, caressing her until the sun turned burning hot and the hands started to undress her and…

And, then, she would wake up.

She wasn't sure if she was relieved or disappointed that she woke up. All she had wanted to do was escape from her past, and now here it was, following her! Plus, she faced a future, which looked as heartbreaking as the last time. This was not a good situation to be in.

After taking a cold shower, so as to not remind her of the fiery meadow, Emma felt more relaxed. So what if she liked kissing Jules? It was no big deal. It wasn't like anything serious was going to happen between them, and no one was close enough to them to see through the lie.

Emma smiled, feeling more satisfied with her life.

As she walked out of her bathroom, Emma noticed the smell of lilacs. Its strong scent stopped her in her tracks. She knew that odor; she had memorized it.

There, sitting on her bed, looking like she'd just flown in from Paris, or Milan, was Becca: Emma's tall, bouncy friend, and one of the few people who might see straight through the lie.

Emma sighed, "Oh shit."

15

"Becca? What are you doing here?"

"Well it's good to see you too, Emma, my disappearing best friend!"

Emma forced her mouth to close and thought of something she could tell her. For some reason, Emma didn't want to tell Becca about Luke. Maybe it was because she's spent most of her time over the past few months gushing about how much she loved him, or, maybe, it was because, in the back of her mind, Emma wondered whether Becca even cared. She probably wouldn't even see the problem with Luke using her as payment to a debt that her recently widowed father had against his family. At least he was hot.

Emma sighed inwardly; it seemed like no one cared, or thought it was a big deal. They all made her feel like a whiney little girl, except Julian. She mentally slapped herself again.

"No, of course I'm happy to see you, I'm just... surprised! You're in London?" Emma said with a half-smile.

"Of course I'm in London, silly. When I heard that you

were here, I came straight away," Becca said as she flipped her curls over her shoulder and wandered to Emma's closet.

"What? How did you know I was here?" Now Emma was confused. Anyone would think she's been blogging about her runaway destination, or broadcasting it on nationwide television; it was so easy to find her.

Becca laughed. "It wasn't a great secret, honey. Although, I must say, I was quite bummed when I found out you'd left without telling me. I mean, when Luke called, I was all, 'What the frick, Emma!' And—"

"What? Luke called you? Why would Luke call you?" Emma practically shouted.

"Why wouldn't he? He was really worried about you— something about you running away from him and hooking up with some random loser in London. I was so concerned. Of course, I told him it couldn't be true; you loved Luke so much. I mean, imagine you doing something so horrible to poor Luke—"

"Actually, I did leave Luke."

Becca's brown eyes widened as she looked away from Emma's wardrobe. "What? How could you do that? You were obsessed with him."

"I was not obsessed with him! I just—I thought we had something good together." Emma thought about saying she had loved him before remembering that Julian had told her that she had never actually loved him. "I was wrong about him. We weren"t what I thought."

"Well, gosh," Becca said, walking around the bed to hug her. "That must have been horrible for you, sweetie."

Emma returned the embrace. Maybe Becca would understand. "Yeah, it really was. I felt like everyone had been lying to me and—"

"Wait though! The other thing he said wasn't true was it? You haven't come to London to hook up with some loser rebound have you?"

"Well I…" Emma started.

"Because I told Luke I thought that was just stupid. I mean, you never really dated anyone; you were like a dating saint, and, honestly, all the girls were so surprised when you hooked up with Luke because he was so hot, and no guy had ever paid you any attention before, not that you ever cared, but, still, it was a relief. So, when Luke said you had another guy here I was like, no way."

Emma let her finish, her eyebrows going up into her hair.

It was true that she hadn't dated much back home. It wasn't that she was a prude, like all her friends had thought, Emma had never felt a connection with anyone, except Luke. She supposed that guys hadn't been lining up around the block for her, but there had been some interested in her over the years; it was always overshadowed by the kind of worship that her friends, like Becca, with their skyscraper legs and sexy attitudes seemed to get. Emma had never been bitter about it, until now.

She had been going to tell Becca the truth about Jules, but now Emma relished the thought of seeing her face when Becca saw just how out of her league Emma's new boyfriend was.

"Well there is a new guy." Emma watched Becca's face contort with horror before disbelief took hold. "Becca he's just great!"

Emma gushed with a big fake smile on her face. "I never told you about him before because I thought I was never going to see him again, and it just hurts too much to think about it, but as soon as I found out that Luke was a complete scumbag, I knew that Jules and I should be together."

"Jules?" Becca's face brightened, but still looked suspicious. "Don't get me wrong, sweetie, it's not that I'm not happy for you, but I care about you. Don't you think you should come home and forgive poor Luke, and forget about this … ahem… new guy?"

Emma's eyes narrowed. Becca didn't believe her. She loved her friend, but Emma swore that sometimes she just wanted to strangled some sense into her.

A knock sounded on the door and Emma jumped as she heard Jules' voice call her name. She smiled at Becca. "That's him right now."

Becca returned the grin. "I can't wait to meet him."

16

Suspicion wafted over Jules when he saw Emma staring at him, and her pleased smile, not to mention that as she did so, she looked like a warrior, sex, angel goddess.

"What's wrong?" Jules asked.

Emma's smile just broadened and Jules noticed for the first time the sarcasm in it.

"Julian! I've missed you."

"Have you?" he asked with a smirk.

Emma did some, not too subtle, head jerking towards something in her room and he guessed that there was someone there that needed lying to. Man, they were going to have to work on her acting.

That's okay, a voice in the back of his head said, *that's just another chance to spend time with her.*

"Someone here?" he mouthed.

She nodded her head and stuck out her hand.

Jules smiled down at it. Emma huffed and whispered, Take my hand, jerk-face."

He chuckled to himself and wound his hand with hers,

noticing how soft and warm it was, Jules had the sudden impulse to never let go of it.

"Becca!" Emma called out. "There's someone I want you to meet."

Becca? Not Luke? And why was she so keen all of a sudden to introduce him?

His questions remained unanswered as a tall girl with brown curls the draped her face bounced around the corner. At first Jules thought this new arrival was Emma's sister, but while this girl was no doubt pretty, she had none of that casual grace and slap in the face gorgeousness which Emma possessed.

The girl, Becca he presumed, had seen something that shocked her. While she had skipped into the room with a little smile, Jules saw the smile drop from her face as she froze on the spot. She stared at him before jerking her head towards Emma, then turned back to Jules. Becca screamed.

Julian pulled Emma behind him. Oh, God, his fans had started getting keys to his hotel now?

Emma pushed herself back in front of him and walked closer to the girl, who now hyperventilated, which was only slightly better than screaming. "Becca," she said with a smile, "I'd like you to meet Julian. Julian, my friend from back home, Becca."

Julian raised an eyebrow but caught on quick. He reached out his hand, which she took with a trembling one. "Nice to meet you."

"Wow, it's so—so—I mean—wow, Emma, you didn't tell me it was Julian Brex!"

Emma's smile broadened and Jules wondered whether

they really were friends. "I told you I was with someone. I didn't think it mattered who he was."

Jules stared at her; even if she was being sarcastic, that was still a pleasant thing for him to hear. He forgot about Becca and moved behind Emma, wrapping his arm around her waist and bringing her up against his chest.

"Have you told her, yet, love?" he whispered in her ear.

"Told her what?" Emma asked, her breathing a little faster.

Jules grazed his lips along her jaw and down the side of her throat. "That we're engaged."

"What?! Engaged?!" Becca jumped in.

Emma recovered and looked at her friend. "That's right. When things ended with Luke I realized that this is where I wanted to be and we didn't want to waste any time."

Becca looked dazed, but she didn't say anything for several minutes and Jules just pressed himself closer to Emma.

"That's... um... great. Congrats, babe, I'm so happy for you!" Her smile was so bright, Jules almost believed she was sincere.

"So, Julian," Becca said turning to him with a different kind of smile, "Did you and Emma have any plans for tonight? Cause I think you and I should have dinner. I've got to get to know the man my best friend is marrying."

Jules felt Emma try to launch herself from his arms, so he quickly pulled her back, and said, "Actually, Emma and I are going to a little gathering tonight."

Emma turned to face him. "We are?" she asked, carefully.

"Yep."

"Oooo, what is it?" Becca chimed in. "Maybe I could come too."

"It's the MTV music awards and, no, you can't come." He looked back down at Emma and said, "Sorry. I can only take one date."

Emma scowled at him, forgetting that Becca was there. "You might have given me some more notice? It's four o'clock and I don't have anything to wear."

"Sorted." Jules said with a smile and Emma noticed for the first time the black garment bag that was flung over one of his shoulders. "And your hair and makeup will be up in an hour."

With another smile, that Jules knew would get her heart pumping, he nodded at Becca and left. He couldn't wait to see how Emma looked that night, almost as much as he couldn't wait to see how she punished him for springing this on her.

What could he say? Her punishment was the sweetest kind.

17

An hour after Becca had left, Emma perched on the edge of her bed, her mind blown.

Honestly, she expected little bits of brain to be on the walls behind her.

Yes, Jules had sprung this on her, and, yes, she intended to castrate him when it was all over—I mean, even a girl like Emma, who preferred jeans over skirts and wore minimal makeup, still needed some time to get ready for an awards show; yet, even though he had done yet another spontaneous thing, and something that could blow apart their little ruse, right now, he was her favorite person.

He had gotten her a dress, but not just any dress, possibly the most beautiful, yet trendy, and amazing dress she had even set eyes on. The dress was a deep plum purple, with a thick, jeweled top half, which managed to make her lack of cleavage look full and enticing, but not trashy. To say that the fabric was soft was an understatement; when Emma put it on, she felt like someone had enveloped her in silk-laden, velvet robe that caressed and hugged her skin--not a stifling choke, but a protective embrace. The gown split apart from the slit that ran up the side of her left leg, allowing it to drag slightly, making her appear more like royalty than just a rock star's date. Emma stared at herself in the floor length mirror, not believing that Julian knew her well enough to choose the dress she dreamed of wearing.

The people who came and did her hair and makeup were so fast and silent, Emma had almost forgotten they had come at all, but the evidence that they had existed, and not some daytime hallucination of hers, was evident in her face: her skin looked flawless with a luminescent glow, the eyes big, smoky, and seductive, while the lips had been shaded a pale pink. Her hair, which was usually wore shoulder length and loose, had been tousled and thrown up into a half up, half down contraption that added a glossy, and elegant, touch.

Looking at herself in the mirror now, Emma had to admit that she looked beautiful; there was a new, strange fluttering in her pulse, and tightening in her stomach, which she couldn't make sense of. A second later a loud, cocky knock rattled the door and Emma reminded herself to take a slow, deep breath before answering taking care not to trip in the heels as she was unused to wearing them.

When the door swung open, Emma's breath caught in her throat. If the sight of Julian in jeans was heartbreaking, then Julian in a tuxedo was enough to make Emma feel as though she had ripped her own heart out of her chest and handed it to him. He was too sexy to handle. Far too good-looking for her newfound glamor to even stand a chance against. She released the breath that had lodged in her lungs, and realized that he wasn't moving either.

Jules hadn't gasped, or expressed how beautiful she looked, and how all he wanted to do was pull her back inside that hotel room and stare at her all night, instead of going to the awards. No, he had just stopped, and stared.

Emma felt a moment of insecurity wash over her as she wondered whether she was meant to look differently, before remembering why she was there and who he was. She didn't need to impress him.

"What?" she asked with a scowl.

"Nothing." He motioned her out the door.

Emma stormed out, upset that he didn't seem to think she looked nice.

"Are you okay?" he asked in the elevator.

"Fine," she snapped, though it was a lie.

She could almost feel his absurd heat, even though they were as far apart as the small elevator would allow, and she smelled him again, that tantalizing, beckoning cologne that made her want to throw herself at him. Emma pressed herself into the cool, wooden wall and as far away from that heat and smell as she could. Jules had other ideas. In one quick stride he crossed the space and pulled Emma to his side.

"Hey-" she protested.

Jules interrupted her. "Shh. The show, remember?"

Emma frowned. This show was getting harder and harder to act. Emma swore that when they entered the lobby, every single head turned their way, including Luke, who sat, stony faced, at the bar with a smiling Becca by his side. They laughed when Emma and Julian came in sight before clamming up. Awed, Becca smiled, whether at Emma's dress, or Julian's butt, Emma couldn't tell; but Luke only had eyes for her. He looked her up and down; desire filled his greedy eyes.

Well – at least someone thought she looked good.

Emma scowled up at Julian whose smile was more strained than usual, but his hand was just as warm. *Geez*, she wondered, *what was wrong with him?* Emma thought he did this kind of thing every other day. A new event, a new dress, a new girl.

Just as she saw Luke rise from his chair, Julian shot him a deadly glare and propelled Emma towards the exit, which she noticed was lined with security this time, keeping the massive crowd at bay. Emma sighed in relief; she didn't know how capable she would be of beating off crazy groupies in a dress and stilettos.

Julian didn't even glance at them; he didn't wave, smile, or sign autographs like he did every other time. He put a firm hand on the small of Emma's back and half carried her into the waiting Bentley.

Once inside, and speeding away, Emma shuffled as far from him as possible and looked out the window. Great! Now he barely spoke to her and manhandled her. Julian's deep sigh behind her caught her attention.

"You look beautiful Emma," he said.

Emma spun around to glare at him, but the hunger in his gray, eyes which shone as they took in every detail on her face, stopped her. The silence stretched on for two minutes before Julian cried, "Dammit!" and threw an arm around Emma's waist, pulling her to his side.

After her pulse recovered, Emma turned to him with a raised eyebrow.

"Explain?" she said.

Julian remained quiet for a moment. "I want—just stay close to me tonight, okay?"

Emma wanted to say no, that he could stay close to himself but chose not to. Instead, she just looked away from those bright eyes and murmured, "Okay."

18

If Emma hadn't already known that Jules was bad for her, she would have been convinced as soon as she stepped out of their car. Julian got out first and smiled at something a reporter had said. Emma could guess what it was as the plush interior of the Bentley muffled the man's statement. She knew it would be a big crowd; she knew to expect screaming girls and paparazzi, but when Jules reached back a moment later for her hand, Emma watched as his face caught the last rays of the afternoon sun, and wished to dive headlong inside the car.

The red carpet bore more of a resemblance to blood— like the blood all these girls barely contained by a thin side rope imagined spilling from her in torrents—than one of luxury. Panic filled her.

Jules looked sideways at his date. It wasn't the first time he'd brought a date to one of these things, but they were always rehearsed actresses and models used to this sort of treatment and got a kick out of them. One look at Emma's horrified face made him realize that she was far from amused, and more terrified for her own life. If she didn't look so comical, her eyes wide like dinner plates, her lips parted in a perfect O, then Julian might have been concerned for her, but he only chuckled and reached out to wind her hand into his, the tension from earlier forgotten.

Emma exhaled as she looked up at Julian. It was strange how his touch had that kind of effect on her, that it instantly calmed her even when she was on the verge of an anxiety attack. Emma reminded herself that it was probably only because her body registered that she now had an old veteran at her side who would be able to guide her through this no problem. At least, she thought there was no problem, as she looked at his god-like face, shining as he chuckled; he seemed happier now. Emma still did not understand what had happened in the limo.

Suddenly, they were propelled forward. Emma was pulled along, securely, at Julian's side as they posed for what seemed to be an endless slew of photos. At one point when Jules leant down to whisper in her ear to smile, the cameras went haywire and the shrieks from the crowd reached a crescendo.

Jules greeted some of the fans, skilfully keeping them from stroking his face and ripping off his clothes like they tried to do time and time again. Emma had to be patient in these moments, and remind herself to not jump forwards and push them all away like she wanted to. Once again, she remembered that she couldn't blame them for their obsession with Julian, especially when he wore his tux and was more than handsome.

By the time they made it inside, Emma's head spun and she had melded herself to the strength of Julian's side.

In front of her, was a sight that took her breath away, but didn't help her anxiety. The old theater was more grand and decorative than anything Emma had seen in her life—and she stayed at the Ritz! She admired the intricate roof lining, the hardwood floors that had seen however many centuries of history, and she stared with disbelief at the huge plasma TVs and laser lights, which had been attached to the walls for the awards ceremony.

The people inside were just as glamorous and twice as intimidating. Celebrities flittered by her like people pushing past each other in a mall at Christmastime; she caught a glimpse of Zac Efron smiling at photographers, his girlfriend standing behind him. Emma saw Rachael from *Friends* walk over and hug the guy who played King Arthur, and saw the Jonas Brothers playing imaginary air-guitars, looking like douche bags. She never cared for them.

They all stopped to talk to Julian. Timberland came up, gave him a quick slap on the back and whispered something in his ear, which made him smile before disappearing into the crowd with his entourage. Emma Watson bounced up and kissed him on both cheeks before looking suspiciously at Emma. This seemed to happen each time someone greeted them: the celebrities walked up, smiled at Julian like a long lost brother (or lover in the case of the girls) and glowered at Emma like she had snuck in a back door.

Jules didn't seem to notice. Every time he greeted them and presented Emma; some revealed their dislike for her presence, while others smiled at her when they realized she was meant to be there. Usher kissed her on the cheek and the guy from *Death Cab For Cutie* told her, in his shy way, that she looked beautiful. As the evening progressed, Emma relaxed, but still felt that, at any moment, a security guard was going to come and hoist her over his shoulder, and put her back outside with the regular people. Emma began to realize why Jules was so cocky. They all loved him; everyone outside had been screaming for Julian. It was annoying.

Julian guided them to their table and pulled out Emma's chair for her with a smile. She looked at him suspiciously.

"What?" she asked.

"What?" he questioned back.

"Why are you looking at me like that?" She put her hands on her hips and he only pulled the chair out a little further.

"I'm just wondering if you're having a good time?" Emma sank down into the chair and one of his hands brushed her collarbone; she couldn't tell if it was an accident.

"I—I suppose I am. I guess I don't really know what I'm supposed to do here." She looked at him as he moved into his own chair. "I mean, am I really just supposed to stand beside you and smile?"

"That's all I do here. All anyone does. You just have to see it as an opportunity. That's what I do."

"An opportunity to what?" Emma asked with a smirk as a waiter put some champagne on their table. "To mingle? To promote myself? In case you haven't noticed, superstar, I'm not really keen on publicity."

Jules raised an eyebrow. "An opportunity to learn, actually. Everyone has something worth knowing; even the dullest person in the universe will know something you don't. So," he said, leaning into her and stroking the back of her hand with a finger. "I suggest you shut up and start learning."

Emma stared at him. His gray eyes mocked her, but held an underlying strength which seemed to pulse as much as her skin under his finger, which created havoc with her concentration. "Oh," was all she said.

For most of the night, they sat together at their little table, talking quietly and chatting with whomever came up to talk to Julian. He pointed out funny things about the people around them, telling Emma stories about some of the crazy things that had happened to him at these kinds of events. He told her that, so far, this had been the most tame awards show of his life. Emma looked up at the gymnasts hanging from the roof and told him that she didn't think she'd be able to handle one of his rowdy nights.

He just chuckled.

It was in the middle of one of the presentations that someone came up and tapped Julian on the shoulder, subtly, and he stood up.

"Where are you going?" Emma asked.

"I have to perform. It won't take long." He smiled.

Her eyes narrowed. "And you didn't think to tell me this sooner?"

"Nope." He smiled again. "I didn't think it was important." And then he was gone.

Emma huffed, every time she started thinking he was decent he would go and act like a little shit again. *It was a good thing he was attractive*, she thought as she watched him walk on stage and sit at the piano. The spotlight hit his face and she drew in a breath. *Very attractive!*

The crowd roared and squealed at the sight of him, but went dead silent as the first notes of the piano echoed through the hall. Emma too, felt her own heart jump a little as Jules leant into the microphone and said quietly, "This is a new song." He chuckled. "A very new song, actually. But it's special."

With that, he started playing, and Emma was instantly struck by the music; the soft, romantic, but strong melody from the piano. Soon, the music was taken over by his voice, which was more beautiful than any instrument.

Emma went dead still as she listened.

Hello midnight eyes,
Brighter than the stars
More than anything before you
Welcome midnight my new sun
My endless light and razor tongue
More lovely than anything
More wicked than the worst thing
She's so lovely
She's so painful
I hope I survive her.
Midnight my new sun,
Brighter than the old one
I'll see you
In every happy smile
In every lustful desire
In everything real,

There you'll be midnight
Oh blue just fade away,
My burning midnight girl
My burning midnight sun
Brighter than anyone
Midnight I'm in love,
If you weren"t real
Then I'd make you up.

There was silence. After the song, the last strains of the piano died away and Emma didn't even dare to breathe. The applause broke out, raging and cheering, but Emma still didn't move.

Midnight eyes?

Julian stood up to take a bow and she caught his eye. He didn't blink and his gray eyes didn't waver from her own. He smiled, to the collective sigh of the female audience and walked off stage.

Oh God. Emma thought.

The last lines of the song played over and over in her mind. "Midnight I'm in love…"

He loved her? What should she do now? *Oh I know*, she thought, *I'll pass out.*

19

Emma didn't pass out, she wished that she could have had that release. Instead, she sat there, gawking and gaping like a moron as the stares around her slowly turned from curiosity to a general wonder if she was mentally ill.

Emma Roberts came up to her, put one hand on either side of her chair and looked her in the face. Her mouth went into a firm frown as she scrutinized her eyes. Leaving with a quick "Dammit!"

Emma sighed. Did she think her eyes were midnight? Is that why she left? Oh god oh god oh god.

"Hey." Came a deep voice at her ear.

"Jesus!" Emma cried as she jumped in shock.

Jules laughed as he kissed her cheek. "So, what did you think?"

Emma's eyes widened in horror. "I…uh…nice song."

Jules raised an eyebrow, and for a moment, Emma thought she'd offended him, but then he replied, "Thank you. I'm glad you think so."

She wasn't lying; it was a beautiful song. She would have loved it even if it had been sung by some ugly, random guy. Emma was already trying to commit it to memory; she never wanted to forget the soft piano, the firm, deliberate voice, and the lyrics saying over and over the sweetest things she'd ever heard, the sweetest and the best…

"Anyway," she said, breaking her thoughts, "um, when did you write it?"

"A while ago."

"Oh." Emma rethought her approach. She needed to find out if it was about her! "It's just—you said it was very new."

"A couple of weeks old is very new.

"Oh." Emma sighed.

A couple of weeks. It wasn't about her.

Emma smiled brightly, then quickly sunk into a frown.

Julian watched her reaction; he couldn't tell her, not yet. It would just freak her out. Look at her right now, her beautiful face twisted in between frowning and worry as she chewed her lip and lowered her eyebrows. Jules almost groaned aloud. Of course the song was about her! How many girls with eyes the color of midnight did she think he knew? Jesus, this was getting complicated.

He had always planned on telling her of course. Jules had thought it would be funny to watch the panic in her face, but see the desire and satisfaction in her eyes—it had gone all wrong. He hadn't meant to say he loved her; that had been improvised. He was going to end with something funny, something to make her smile, but the words had come out before he could stop them. Jules didn't mean it of course, it just fit well with the song.

He frowned now.

They didn't stay long at the awards, only to accept his

awards (4 in total) and politely decline frenzied invitations to a dozen after parties.

Emma had smiled the whole time, but there was a tension there, more than just the blatant dislike from before. She was wary of him now, cautious.

He looped his arm around hers on the way into the hotel and sighed. It felt good to be near her again; he had kept his distance at the awards, and in the car, and it had cost him. Jules might not love her, but he wasn't an idiot. He definitely liked her, and wanted her.

My god did he want her!

For once, Emma didn't pull away from him when they entered the elevator. She just stayed with his arm around her waist and a frown on her face.

Julian looked down at her. He saw her bite her lip again and smile an awkward smile.

That's it, he thought; making a decision. As soon as they were back in the hotel room he was going to tell her. Tell her the song was about her and that he liked her enough to be with her. She would be grateful and admit that she liked him, too. Then he would kiss her like he's wanted to kiss her from the first moment he saw her.

That's it, planned solved. Julian Brex was no coward!

They were about two steps from her hotel door and Jules' ultimate fantasy when a deep voice called from down the hall.

"Amanda." The icy voice forced Jules to stand straighter, his arm tightening on Emma's waist.

Emma stiffened and peeked around him; her eyes widened and her bottom lip quivered. "Father!"

20

Emma froze. Oh god, she was dead. She didn't know if she could pull off lying to her father, especially now that she didn't think she'd be able to lie with Julian next to her, quite like she used to; something had definitely shifted there.

"Amanda," he father answered in a quiet voice.

Her entire body shivered. Julian's arm went from around her waist to squeezing her hand.

Her father noticed the movement. "I'd like to talk to you, please." It wasn't a question.

Emma nodded and walked towards him with Julian.

"In private," said her father.

Jules looked at her with a worried expression. Whether he was worried for her, or for what her father could do to him, Emma wasn't sure.

"I'll be fine," she whispered to him.

Jules wanted to argue, but chose to run his fingers down her cheek instead and nodded before continuing to his room.

Emma tried to control her breathing as she walked up

to her father, meeting his gaze as he led her into a nearby suite. She had to remind herself that she had nothing to apologize for. Emma stood straighter as she noticed the other people in the room. "I thought you said in private," she said, matching her father's icy tone.

Her father stared at her. "Luke has a very important part in what we need to discuss; and Becca just showed up."

Emma narrowed her eyes at Luke. "Whatever," she said and stood by the window, watching the rain that had just started to fall. *Typical.*

She realized that she still wore her dress and shivered. Emma thought that if Julian was here he'd give her his jacket, or at least put an arm around her. She looked over at Luke as he undressed her with his eyes, knowing that would never do anything kind for her.

Julian may be an arrogant A-hole who wrote songs that made her think he loved her, but then turned out they were just about some random girl whom he wrote about a few weeks ago, but wasn't in the picture anymore, even though he said he loved her—she took a deep breath—but at least he was a gentleman.

"What?!" she snapped at Luke.

He grinned at her, the grin that was once the center of her universe, but hardly made a flutter now.

Emma looked to her father. He stared down at her his expression so dark and remote that she almost didn't recognize him. Where was her loving father? Where was the man who had treated her like the most special thing in his universe for the last 18 years?

"Father," she said, squaring her shoulders. "Why have you come here?"

He raised an eyebrow. "My only child abandons her fiancée and runs half way across the world—was I meant to stay at home?"

"Yes, you were. Although given the… circumstances, I can understand how you're reluctant to let your meal ticket get away." Emma had never spoken to her father like that in her life, and the look of disbelief shone on his face.

It was Becca who answered. "Oh, Emma, we were all so worried about you. Your father called me straight away to find out where you were." She looked at him, frightened herself. "Of course, that was before I knew, sir."

"Hush, Rebecca." Her father took a deep breath and turned to Emma again. "I suppose you are justified in being upset. It was wrong of me to place you in that situation and I am sorry."

Emma's mouth gaped and Luke jumped to his feet.

"What? Sir, you know she must marry me."

Her father kept his gaze on Emma. "But, while I am sorry, you must marry Luke now. You, and therefore this family, have given his family their word, and we do not back out on our word."

"Watch me," came Emma's defiant response.

"Amanda, you are coming home and you are going to marry Luke."

Luke smiled now, like the devil he was.

"I am not. Father, there is nothing you can do to make me come with you, short of dragging me to the plane yourself ,and I warn you that if that's the case, I have the police on speed dial."

Her father took one step towards her. "There must be a marriage!"

"Oh, but she's engaged again," Becca chimed in, "didn't you know."

He looked surprised, his bushy eyebrows raising. "Luke mentioned that you had attached yourself to someone new; he said nothing about an engagement."

"Because that is irrelevant!" Luke burst in. "It does not matter how many jackoffs Emma attaches herself to. If it's not me, then there's no deal, old man!"

"Oh, fuck off, Luke." Emma growled. "And if by 'deal' you're referring to my father paying back the debt against your family, I think you will find that any money should work the same. Not that it matters, I have no intention of giving you anything."

Luke turned to face her, his irate eyes boring into hers. "You would leave your father to suffer?" he asked.

Emma flushed. She could never do that. It didn't matter how much he had hurt her, she couldn't just abandon him, and Luke knew it. "No, I couldn't. Which is why I am marrying Julian. I am certain, if I remember the terms of my grandfather's will, that any marriage will secure me the money."

Luke took a menacing step towards her. "Over my dead body!" he screamed.

Emma closed the distance between them. "Gladly!"

"Enough!" her father's deep voice cut in. "Luke, Becca, out. I would like to speak to my daughter alone."

Luke scowled as he stomped out the door, while Becca smiled as though she'd been at a birthday party, instead of a family feud.

Her father took a deep breath and rubbed his temples. "Why are you doing this Emma? You love Luke."

Her eyes widened. "No, I don't. I could never, now that I know that everything about us was manufactured. How could you do that? How could you lie to me? Sell me?"

"Stop being so dramatic!" He whipped around. "We are going home, tonight! I've already ordered the jet."

"Then you will be wasting a lot of fuel for just you. I'm staying here."

"For what? What are you staying for Emma? For weather that you hate, for a city you don't know, for friends you don't have? Or, were you expecting me to believe that you were staying for that fake fiancée of yours?"

Emma almost gasped. "Wha—I—uh—"

"Did you really expect me to believe that if you won't marry Luke, a boy you've been in love with since you were sixteen, then you would come to London and get engaged in a day?"

The grim line that stretched across her father's mouth held a hint of victory that drove Emma insane.

"Jules is special." She knew she meant it as she said it.

"So, he is going to be your entire life, then? What about college, is that just not happening now? And what happens when this new boy turns out to have a fault, when he hurts you are you going to run half way around the world from him?"

"Julian isn't like that! He wouldn't lie to me like Luke did."

"You thought that about Luke at the start too."

"Why are you taking no responsibility for this? You practically sold me to pay off your debts! Well you know what, I lost mom as well and I wish she could see what you've become!"

Her father slapped her. For the first time in her life, her doting father had struck her.

Emma stomped out the door and ran as soon as it closed behind her, her heels clomped on the carpeted floor. She pounded on the door she needed, so close to tears that she whimpered.

She'd be okay, he would make everything okay. Then she wouldn't have to think about what her father had said, about the things she knew she's been putting off thinking about.

The door opened and Emma launched herself into his arms. They closed around her without a word and so tight that Emma was sure he would crush her. She pulled him closer.

"Julian." She murmured. "I need you."

21

They held each other remained locked in the embrace be Jules. moved them over to the couch against the window, still not saying a word, and sat them down; still wrapped around each other, just watching the lights of London flicker on and off as it dawn approached.

Emma felt like she was trying to memorize him. His thunderstorm smell and the way his muscular arms held her gently. It was so easy with him, she realized; so easy to ignore all the terrible things she wished to escape and didn't want to think about. Emma kept telling herself, just tonight. They could have just tonight to be with each other without remembering all of the other stuff, and tomorrow they would talk and make sense of why it felt so good to be with each other. Tomorrow they would, but not tonight. Tonight was theirs.

Jules had never seen Emma like this. It was like she had let down all of her walls and she'd never been more beautiful to him. He wondered what had happened. Jules couldn't count the amount of girls who had arrived to him, blubbering and in emotional crisis—he'd never cared. He'd never given a damn that they were upset. Perhaps, that was cold of him, but he just never cared.

Yet, here he sat wrapped around a girl for hours. It should have been awkward, but it wasn't. It was perfect, and when her eyelids started to droop as the sky lightened, Jules suggested that she go to bed. His heart overflowed as she shook her head and led him into his bedroom.

He left while she got changed, slipping off her dress and taking out her hair, putting one of his t-shirts over her underwear. Jules laughed at himself when he realized that his hands were shaking. She smiled at him when he came back in and climbed under the sheets, patting the space beside her. There was nothing suggestive about that; she just wanted him near her. Jules ceased quivering and obeyed Emma's wish, climbing in beside her and Emma tucked herself in around him. He wrapped one arm over her shoulders and the other in her hair.

"Goodnight," she whispered, her dark blue eyes shining.

"Sweet dreams," Jules said back.

Wrapped around each other, both feeling more than they knew, they fell asleep.

A few hours later, Emma woke up alone. She groaned and rolled over. Where was he?

This bed looked like hers, but it smelled different; it had a man's scent.

Emma sat up and glanced down at the top she wore over her underwear. "Uh!" she said, pulling the sheets up and remembered where she was.

Julian had been so good to her last night.

She remembered her silent promise to herself that today they would talk and figure everything out. Suddenly, that was nowhere near as attractive a prospect as just having another day like last night.

Emma lifted the t-shirt up to her nose. It smelt like him. Thunderstorms and peppermint. The best smell in the world.

After walking to the bathroom to check herself out—holy crap!—she looked like a scarecrow—she fixed her appearance and tiptoed to the living room.

Julian stood against the window with a cup of coffee in one hand and the newspaper in the other. Emma stopped when she saw him and drank him in; he was far too gorgeous.

"Morning," she said.

He spun around and smiled at her, thrilled to see her still in her underwear and his t-shirt. "Morning. I ordered you some breakfast. Take a seat."

Jules pointed at the table, which was sagged underneath the weight of everything he could think of to order.

Emma sat down, grabbing some fruit and muesli with a big plate of crispy bacon. "Thanks."

He watched her eat in silence. She was so beautiful, even when her hair was a fluffy mess and she had smudges of last night's makeup caked under her eyes. He wished that he could have been with her when she had woken up. Jules had been pleasantly surprised when he had woken up still wrapped in her arms, only closer than before, if that was possible. Unfortunately, he'd also woken up with a dramatic case of morning wood and thought that it would be better for the situation if he got up and calmed himself, a little.

"So," he begun, as Emma dug into her food, "are we going to talk about what happened last night?"

Emma gulped. "Last night?"

"With your dad? You were pretty upset after talking to him."

Emma relaxed. "Oh," she said, "he wants me to come home."

Jules looked at her for a long moment. "But, you're not going to are you?"

She frowned. "Well, no, but he gave me a lot of things to think about. He—he asked me what I'm doing here, in a place I don't know, with no friends or family or…"

She stopped speaking and Julian realized that she was upset. Her father had rattled her. "What do you mean no friends?" he asked with a smile. "You've got me, haven't you?"

"That's other thing," said Emma, "he said that our engagement was fake."

Julian smile faded. "How would he know that?"

Emma just shrugged. "I don't want to go home," she said, "but I suppose that I just never wanted to think about what I'm doing here, and Luke is…"

Julian's eyes narrowed upon the mention of Luke.

"Luke is more determined than ever. It's like a challenge to him. I thought he would believe us by now."

Julian reached for a glossy magazine and chucked it on the table. "Well this should help convince him."

Emma picked it up. It was a popular tabloid with the

heading reading "JULIAN'S CINDERELLA STORY". Underneath there was a huge blown up photo of Jules and Emma. It was the one from the awards when Julian had leaned down to Emma's ear to tell her to smile, but it looked as though he had brushed her hair aside and kissed her with Emma's head turned towards it with a small, adoring smile on her face.

Emma gasped out loud. They looked like they were a couple. More than that, they looked like they were in love.

"I've already arranged for a copy to go to your father's room with the morning paper. Hopefully, Luke gets a look at it too." Julian looked at her shocked expression.

"Wow, we really look—I mean, wow!"

"Yeah, I know. And don't worry; magazines are great at spinning stories however they want them."

Emma nodded.

"Emma," Jules started, "there's something you should know, too."

Emma looked away from the photo.

"I'm leaving."

Emma's face fell and her heart dropped in her chest. He was leaving? He couldn't; he couldn't just leave. She needed him! She wanted him!

"Oh," she said in a flat tone, looking away from him.

Jules chuckled slightly and Emma glared at him. "No, I'm not leaving you. I'm just leaving the hotel. My apartment is ready." He looked at her surprised face. "You didn't think I lived in a hotel did you?"

"Um, yeah, I kind of did." Emma felt sheepish.

"Nope, I have an apartment near Hyde Park."

"Oh, well, that's nice for you." He was still leaving. Emma began to realize what this meant. No more late night comfort calls, no random moments with him showing up at her door…

"Emma," Jules said, snapping her out of her mental coma with his deep, and husky, voice that she loved, his slight accent thicker than usual, "I want you to come with me."

"Say again?" Emma couldn't believe what he had asked her.

"Move in with me, Emma."

22

Emma had managed to sneak the magazine back to her room as she hastily fled the scene. Thinking back, she realized that she probably over reacted. Jules probably didn't mean move in with him, as in, move in together, but to move in with him so that their little scheme looked more authentic.

That hit her long after she stammered an "I'll think about it" and hightailed it out the door.

Now she sat on her bed with the magazine spread in front of her, still in her underwear and Jules' t-shirt, which she delayed taking off for as long as possible. Emma took a moment to look at the picture on the front of the magazine again. They really did look cute and happy, which was a testament to how good that photographer must be because Emma remembered only feeling terror at that awards show.

She flipped to the article inside. There was a page of pictures here as well. The first was a promotional image of Julian with a guitar propped on his knee, looking like his usual godlike self. There was another of Emma and Julian at the awards show and one of just Emma by herself, with little arrows pointing to places on her dress which said "WOW" and "MISTAKE". Emma squealed with horror as she looked to the bottom of the page and saw that the magazine had somehow got a hold of her senior school photo where she'd been going through a haystack hair phase. The article ended with a picture of her and Julian the first time they had left the hotel to get some dinner. He had held her hand and pulled her through the crowd, while looking back at her and Emma stared back at him, part terrified, part pissed off.

At least, that's how she thought she looked. The magazine had written underneath "The Look of Love".

Emma huffed and read the article.

Yesterday, international superstar Julian Brex broke the hearts of millions as he was seen on his first official outing with his new girlfriend, 18 year-old Emma Corzeica. The couple were seen at the MTV Music Video Awards, both sporting big smiles and loving glances. American born Emma was said to be "obviously smitten" with the rock-star and who could blame her! Voted one of the sexiest men alive for the 3rd year running, 20 year-old Julian is every teen girl's dream catch.

Emma rolled her eyes and once again realized why Jules had such a big head.

Julian's publicist announced the relationship officially yesterday, and hinted that the young lovers were "quite serious", despite the fact that they have only been spotted together in the last week. Sources say that they met last year while Julian was completing his world tour and since Emma arrived in London, they have been living together in the Ritz hotel. But this is far from a boring relationship, with the gossip mill running wild about what enticed Julian to finally settle down! While the rockstar hasn't quite reached playboy status yet, he has in the past been tied to such starlets as Zooey Deschanel, Taylor Swift, and Ashley Olsen.

In a personal interview with sexy Julian, he called the beautiful Emma "Special" and said that she "meant a lot to him." It is also widely speculated that the acoustic love song that Julian performed at the awards was written about his new love. Do we even hear rumors of a baby bump in Emma's young belly? Or is the gossip about their secret engagement true? One thing is for sure; from the looks of it these two have been sporting they are well and truly smitten!

Emma frowned as she read the last line. She was not smitten. She was not! Just a couple of days ago she contemplated running Julian over with her car rather than kissing him

At least, Emma thought, she knew that the pregnancy rumor wasn't true. A strange heat flooded her as she thought about having sex with Julian, about actually surrendering to his kisses and touches which she secretly lived for, but had to say no to because she valued her sanity. If there was one thing that Julian Brex was good at it was messing with Emma's head.

There was a knock on her door and Emma almost jumped out of her skin.

If that was Julian, she didn't know what she'd do. She felt so strange after last night, and after looking at the photos in the article, Emma wasn't sure she'd be able to control herself if she saw him right now.

She stood up and walked towards the knocking.

If Emma opened that door and saw Julian's arrogant, but perfect, face, she thought that she would just have to,,, "Luke! What are you doing here?"

He smiled devilishly at Emma, reminding her that he was quite attractive himself. "I'm bringing you the headlines."

He held up the same glossy magazine that she had just been reading.

"Thanks, but I've already seen them."

"I figured." Luke pushed past her and into the room, picking up a mars bar she had left sitting around and opened it.

He flipped to the pages about her and Jules while munching the candy. "You know I was quite impressed." He looked up and her and raised an eyebrow. "You really are the sweetest couple."

Emma gritted her teeth. "Thanks. I know."

"Which is why you chose him of course."

"Sorry?" she asked.

"For how it looked."

Emma's mouth jaw dropped to the floor.

"Attractive," Luke said please by her expression. "I wonder if we would have looked that in love—" Luke pointed at the magazine. "—if they had gotten us a few weeks ago."

Emma's eyes narrowed. "I doubt it, considering we were never in love."

"You were in love with me."

Emma imagined herself blowing up Luke's head by sticking a grenade in his mouth.

"Oh, don't look at me like that, babe; you know I loved you too."

"Oh, did I? And don't call me babe. I am not a little pig. How dare you say you love me now after everything." She was dangerously close to either crying or throwing Luke through the window and knowing her usual reactions to him it was likely to be the latter.

"Okay," Luke said, throwing his hands up. "You caught me. So I didn't love you; I wanted you. I still want you; isn't that something?"

As he talked, Luke moved closer to her, winding one of his hands in her hair. Emma had been too shocked with sudden rage to think of moving away. "Don't pretend you don't want me too. You used to beg me to kiss you, to be with you."

Emma's face went up in flames as she remembered the way she used to have to persuade him to kiss her. "Exactly, which proves that you only want me now because someone else does."

Luke's hands moved to her collarbone. "I want you

now because you're beautiful and because you're rightfully mine. Parading yourself around with that famous dickhead is just to make me want you more; I know."

Emma shoved him away from her. "Could you be anymore full of yourself?"

"Could you be anymore delusional? Do you really think someone like Julian Brex is actually going to marry you?"

"Why wouldn't he? He loves me."

"Yes, probably. I've seen the way he looks at you, but he won't love you for long." Luke came closer and moved so his lips were almost on hers. "He'll get bored with you soon and then there will only be me left."

"Now who's delusional?" Emma spat, while moving away from him; trying to pretend that she didn't agree with him.

It was only a matter of time before Julian started to wonder why he was putting himself through so much trouble for someone like her, someone who couldn't even admit to herself that she liked him, that she'd fallen in love with him.

23

"Wow," Emma said; her eyes wide like dinner plates.

This was the most amazing place she'd ever seen. A hundred, no, a thousand times nicer than anything she would have expected from a young, bachelor rock star.

"Your house is really, really nice," she said, still looking around.

His deep voice chuckled. "Our place, remember? I'm so glad you came to your senses and decided to move in."

Emma just smiled. "All of a sudden, I am too."

His apartment was in the old part of the city and resembled a house more than an apartment with its two floors, and though narrow, having been built in the 1700s, probably the town house of some wealthy lord back when they all flittered casually from their country to city houses, it was still spacious. Of course it had been redone to fit the 21st century. The bedrooms (two, Emma had made sure of that) now decked out in plush carpet, but everywhere else was left to the old hardwood floors, and modern fixtures had been put in the bathrooms and kitchen. While it had all of the modern comforts like a 50 inch, flat screen TV in the lounge room, washing machine, and even heated towel racks in the bathrooms, it still possessed the old world charm, which made it special: huge, glazed windows, high ceilings, and little window seats to curl up on and read.

Emma was in love, with his house that is. She felt happy, because now she had the excuse that staying here was a thousand times nicer than staying in a hotel for, and she wondered why she had never wanted to leave it.

"What are you thinking?" asked Jules in a quiet voice from right behind her.

Emma sighed. "That this is probably going to be a lot nicer than I expected."

It was true. At first, she had felt like the biggest sell out for agreeing to move in, but Jules had left her a note before he left for an interview, or something, which gave her the address and told her that he had more than one bedroom, so it wasn't like they would be living together like a real couple. He had said that he didn't care either way, but that he thought it would look much better to her family if she was to want to live with him.

Emma sighed, trying to make herself see that this was a good thing, but she still hadn't felt sure about it. If she was being honest with herself, she wasn't sure that she'd be able to control herself if she lived with Julian. Seeing him every morning, smelling that delicious Julian smell on everything, knowing that he slept just a few feet away.

Emma had had to give herself a mental beating after that one, but she still hadn't made up her mind until she went out to lunch with Becca. She remembered that meeting.

Becca had been sickeningly nice to her all morning that Emma had snapped and asked her why she acted like such a snob.

"I just thought that you might have needed a little tender loving care," Becca had replied in her usual self-praising manner, "after I saw someone carrying out all of Julian's bags this morning."

Emma had just gaped at her.

"Oh, you poor thing," Becca had continued, "finding out that another man didn't really care about you. You must be heartbroken."

Emma had gritted her teeth and curled her fingers into fists underneath the table.

She pulled herself back to the present, where she stood next to Julian in the entrance hall of his home.

"Actually, they were just moving his stuff into his new place. Whoops," Emma said, looking carefully at her. "I should say, our new place."

And that had been that. She couldn't back out and say that she wasn't going to move in with him now. Emma had too much pride for that and if it meant sacrificing sleep, and her sanity, so that her family stayed convinced that she couldn't marry Luke, then so be it.

Jules snapped her back to reality as his hands closed on her shoulders, steering her towards another room. One of his hands dipped to the bare skin just below her collar bone and Emma shivered all over. "This is the music room," he said in her ear.

"Wow," was all she managed to say. She could see at least eight different guitars there; a double bass, a grand piano, and an electric drum set and a sound deck for mixing tracks.

She moved out from under his hands and went to look at the kitchen, grabbing a granny smith apple from the counter and chewing it carefully.

"Hungry?" Julian asked. "I thought you went out for lunch."

Emma's eyes narrowed. "I wasn't really in the mood for eating much, then."

"Fair enough."

It was night time, almost ten. They would have done the tour earlier, but Jules had been held up by some artist in crisis at his production studio.

"I would show you the garden," Jules said, coming closer, catching one of her hands in his, "I will tomorrow when its light." He took the apple with his spare hand and took a bite from the other side, his thumb drawing circles on her palm.

Emma moved around him, going to the doors leading outside. "Are there lights outside?" she asked.

"Yeah, they were put in last week."

"Then, show me now," Emma demanded. "I like gardens."

Julian smiled at her as she opened the double doors and walked into the darkness outside, avoiding his gaze and touching him, but not in her usual way. She wasn't just telling him to F off, like she had done for the past week; she blushed and stammered. He wondered what was wrong with her, but he wasn't going to press it too far; as he found her new nervousness sexy.

"Emma," Jules called, as he made his way to the first little path and didn't see her.

Emma didn't reply so he walked further in. It wasn't that big of a garden, but for London standards it was huge. Jules rounded the hedged corner and stopped breathing.

Emma stood in the center of a little paved courtyard, looking around herself smiling and all Jules could think about was how beautiful she was. The gardeners had put white fairy lights in all of the trees and hedges, making Emma look more like some mystical princess than the American with anger management issues. She smiled at him. "I like this garden."

"I like you in this garden."

Emma snickered. "You don't have many flowers though."

"We don't have many flowers," Julian corrected, "and, no, I like trees more, but if you want flowers, we'll get more flowers."

"No," she said, "I like trees too. You can't climb a flower."

Julian smiled to himself, watching her; something stronger than just the usual heave of longing gripped him.

He walked over to her unable to stand it. It was true that at first he'd wanted her because she was a challenge, because he'd had so few people say no to him that he'd forgotten what it was to really want something, but now it was more: she made him smile with something more than just disbelief now. This craving for her started to become an ache which refused to go away. He was too fast for her to pull away. Julian's arms wound around her narrow waist and propelled her into the nearest hedge; so that the fairy lights surrounded her head like a halo. She had time for one quick gasp before he lowered his lips to hers.

Her plump lips parted under his, surrendering to the dizzy strength that already consumed them. His lips and tongue explored her mouth and the fire sprang up in him hot and demanding. Emma's hands went to his chest, exploring him through his t-shirt. Just as his hands began an exploration of their own, Emma let out a frustrated shriek and tore her lips from his.

She was across the courtyard in a second.

Julian looked at her. Angry this time. He knew that she wanted him, burned for him just like he burned for her. Why couldn't she just let go?

"I'm sorry," Emma said, surprising him—since when did she ever apologize?—and continued, "but if we're going to live together I can't—we can't kept doing stuff like that."

Julian took a step towards her.

Her voice broke, "Please, Julian! I can't stand it anymore. Just stop."

Jules sighed with real sadness and a deeper frustration. "Okay."

She looked at him. "Okay." She repeated.

They walked back inside, together. Emma felt the annoyance rolling off of Julian in waves. He was in front of her and she watched with a tightening stomach as his shoulders stiffened like he was going to turn, and then, the muscles relaxed.

The gray shirt clung to his body and Emma had to strain really hard not to look at his perfectly formed butt.

She had no right to turn him down and then spring into fantasies about him a minute later.

She couldn't explain he actions. She knew she wanted him—for Christ's sake, she'd probably go crazy with how much she wanted him, but Emma knew that if she gave in, if she let go of this pretend animosity towards Julian, then Luke would be right: He'd get bored of her; he'd get bored and leave her.

Julian held the door open for her and she moved past him, accidently brushing his chest in the narrow space. Emma had to bite her lip to hold in the groan that threatened to escape. Air hissed through Julian's teeth and Emma thought she saw him roll his eyes.

Just as Julian walked away to another room, not wanting her to follow him, and Emma thought that she might burst into tears, there was a hum, followed by every light in the house going out. Emma stood in the darkness for a moment, unsure of what to do before a warm hand wrapped around hers. She jumped.

"Shhh," came Julian's voice, "just follow me, it must be a blackout."

He led her through the blackness to what she thought was the lounge room, putting her on the couch. He left her for a moment and lit a candle on the mantelpiece with a lighter he'd pulled from his pocket. "Just stay here for a minute okay. I'll be back."

Jules smiled at her with that tantalizing smile before leaving.

The ten minutes which passed without him could have been ten hours for how long they felt. Emma couldn't take it anymore and got up, making her way through the house with the few lights Jules had lit leading up the stairs.

"Jules," she called. It was humiliating to admit that a grown girl was a little afraid of the dark, but she didn't know what else could be making her heart beat this hard.

"In here," his deep voice rang out.

Emma came to a door which Jules had pointed out on the tour as being his bedroom. She could see the light shining out through the little crack left open. Pushing gently, Emma came to a complete stop at what she saw.

Julian bent over lighting what had to be the millionth candlestick in the room. Coming from the darkness of the lounge room and the hall, it was like some beautiful haven from the outside.

Emma studied Julian's face, his long eyelashes casting shadows on his cheeks, his muscles bunching and smoothing as he moved. He was so much more than handsome. Emma realized that he must be here just to torture her, to make her want something she couldn't have.

Jules looked up upon hearing the little sigh escape her lips, despite Emma's best attempts.

"Emma," he said, his voice deep and soft, "are you alright?"

She eyed at him for a long moment, and, without warning, blurted out "Screw it!" Before bounding across the room and pressing her mouth to his.

24

Emma felt like everything had stopped. Time had frozen and all the little worries fizzled away with Emma's last grips on her self-control.

It took her only a moment after she first launched herself at Julian for his shock to melt away and wrap his arms around her with an agonized, satisfied groan. Another moment after that, Emma realized that time had stopped to allow her body to adjust to such an earth-shattering occurrence.

They kissed as they'd never kissed before, deep, their passion for one another dictating it, with Emma at the reigns. She had made the decision to not fight anymore, whether it was her desire for Julian, her hatred, or deeper feelings; Emma didn't care anymore; it was too exhausting to pretend she didn't feel what she felt: heat

Emma opened her eyes from under her haze of the sudden passion to watch as Julian lowered his head to kiss her. His beautiful face so close that every one of his eyelashes brushed her cheek. Their faces fitted each other's, Julian's cheekbones slotting naturally around hers, her plump lips giving way under his harder, more persistent ones.

His eyes opened; his gaze penetrated her with their meaningful and bare glance that Emma gasped as their lips locked, and dropped her head to press her lips to his neck. Jules groaned again and a shiver pulsed through him. Emma smiled against his tanned skin, which glowed from the candle light, and worked her way down his neck: kissing, sucking, and nipping until she reached his collar bone, while her delicate fingers roamed Jules' torso, tracing the line of his jaw, his elongated neck, and the jutting bone. He breathed heavily as she kissed him, his hands pushing her hips into his until his fingers found the bare flesh between her t-shirt and jeans.

A few days ago, Emma would have slapped herself for letting a half whimper escape her because of a single touch from a boy, but Jules was no boy, and she cast aside her old fears as she pushed her hands up under Jules' ivory t-shirt until she touched his smooth, well-muscled chest.

Lips locked, Emma yanked at his shirt in an effort to rip it off. It stuck to his wide shoulders. Aching even more for her, Jules seized the shirt from Emma's grasp and ripped it over his head, tossing it to the ground.

Emma stepped back, marveling at Jules' toned muscles, and the beads of sweat that glistened in the dancing candle-light, feeling like a coil spring twisted in her stomach as she physically ached to feel him.

Watching her reaction, sinful smile lit Julian's face and he reached for her hands, placing her palms to his firm chest.

Emma groaned with pleasure.

"So you've finally realized," he whispered against her earlobe.

"What?" Emma asked.

"What you've been missing."

Emma replied by pressing her soft, plump lips against Jules' in an electrically charged kiss.

His strong hands reached up under her light t-shirt with such persistence that Emma quaked and goose-pimples formed wherever his fingers touched her, lighting a fire beneath her skin, begging for more. He lifted the shirt over her head in one swift move, and to her surprise, Emma didn't feel the least bit embarrassed as he took a step backwards, still holding onto her slender waist, to study her half-naked form. "I've wanted to see you like this again, since that first day."

Emma remembered the day he found her wearing only her peach underwear and wondered why she had been horrified then, when now, all she desired was for him to see her entire form. "How about I show you a little more."

Jules pressed his forehead to hers, taking in her jasmine perfume, while she, in turn, lost herself to the smell of peppermint and a building thunderstorm, as his meaty hands caressed the small of Emma's back, until they reached the clasp of her lacy bra. He fiddled with it for a second, teasing her, tempting her, before snapping it open, allowing the lacy material to glide to the floor as shadows danced upon them. Emma stood before him with her exposed breasts, marveling at how the golden glow of the candles made them come alive, and aroused Jules even more, as the slight bulge in his jeans conveyed. He lifted his hands and touched her chilled flesh, smoothing them over her breasts before wrapping them around her back, pulling her further into his comforting embrace, and lowering his head to kiss her. Jolts of electricity shot through Emma from the passion within his kiss, and her hands moved to his belt, but he stopped her.

With a firm, but surprisingly gentle gesture, Jules moved their hands to her narrow hips and undid her pants (while still locked in the kiss) and slid them down to her ankles as she lifted her bare feet to kick them off. On the way up, Jules planted caressing kisses on her calf, then her thigh, stroking and rubbing before pausing at her waist. He looked up at her and Emma returned his gaze, giving him permission to remove the lace rimmed panties. With his index finger, Jules snapped the elastic band, causing Emma to jerk from arousal. Slowly, he tugged them downward and off of her—for a brief moment Emma wished she had remembered to wax the little spot of hair that dotted her treasure—and rose to his feet, all the while stroking her skin, teasing her nether area, before straightening to his full height.

Standing naked before him, Emma jumped on him, forcing her lips upon his and wrapping her legs around his waist, squeezing tight, telling him that she desired—no!—needed him. Jules, placed his hand beneath the curve of her buttocks, cradling her as he carried her to the bed. They sank into the pillow-topped mattress as it folded around them, their lips never parting. Both pairs of hands grasped and pulled at the other desperate to be connected, never wanting to let go.

He cupped her firm breasts, squeezing, teasing the nipples as they perked beneath his fingers, before he buried his face in the soft mounds, licking and kissing, while slipping his forefingers into the folds of the flesh between her legs, rubbing, feeding her desire for more. Before he had given her too much, Emma's hands flew to his belt and ripped it free of his jeans. She undid the button and yanked them off of him, releasing him.

Emma opened herself up for Jules, allowing him entrance as he slipped inside of her, pulsing, thrusting, causing her to cup her hands around the firm muscles of his behind and push him further into her. Locked together as one, Jules jerked back and forth inside of Emma, his one desire, while she remained open on the bed, her hands gripping the sheets from the ecstasy that spurned through her. Jules gripped Emma's breasts again, squeezing hard while pushing deeper inside of her, ready to burst from the passion and...

The explosion inside of Emma coursed through her body as Jules released himself, fulfilling Emma's, and his, desire since the day he had seen her in her peach underwear. He relaxed, and locked together in their lover's embrace, each fell asleep beneath the dancing candlelight, oblivious to the night's worries, comforted in their love.

25

"So," Emma said, while shoveling her eighteen-hundredth spoon of honeycomb ice-cream into her mouth, "start again, you were telling me about this new band. What's their name, Beauty Con? Sally Con?"

Jules chuckled into her ear. "Master Con. They're really good actually—kind of an Indie Strokes."

"Cool."

The clock struck eight as the faint sunlight spilled through the slit in the semi-sheer curtains. During the night, while they slept, the blackout ended and the lights came back on, but Jules had gotten up and turned them off again, preferring the atmosphere of the candle-light, and hoping to preserve the magic they had created between him and Emma.

Now she lay against his bare chest, more comfortable than she'd ever been in her entire life, shoving spoonfuls of honeycomb cereal into her mouth. Emma had no desire to discuss the previous night's events, glad to have finally admitted to herself the attraction, and love, she felt towards Jules, and hoped he still felt the same about her.

"Hey!" she shrieked as Jules kissed her forehead before and stole her spoon, dipping it in the tub of chocolate chip ice-cream in his hands.

"What about you?" he asked, "What were you planning to do before you decided to flee to Europe?"

Emma's brow crinkled for a moment. "I guess—I suppose I was planning on going to college, after I married Luke and everything."

"But not anymore?" Jules said, running his hand down her arm.

"No, not anymore."

"Why not?"

"I'm a little…displaced right now; not to mention that all of the college's I wanted to go to are way out of my price range now, unless I want to go ahead and get married for real."

"What college's did you want to attend?"

Emma sighed, all of her childhood dreams of college and independence seemed a distant memory now.

"I was accepted on early admittance to Dartmouth; it was always where I thought I wanted to go, but now…I don't know if I'd be able to just go home."

"Hmm," Jules murmured, his beautiful mouth pouting. "You know, I go to university."

"You do?" Emma asked, looking at him with surprise.

"Yep. Bachelor of Business and Music Production."

"How—how do you even manage that?"

Jules laughed. "It's not without effort I assure you, but it's worth it in the end."

"Well, what university are you at?"

"Oxford."

Emma's mouth dropped, glad that she wasn't facing him anymore. How was it possible that he was gorgeous and a secret genius? He was fast becoming the perfect man and Emma wasn't sure if she should believe it.

She shrugged off the thought. "Oh, well," she said, "I suppose I have to go home sometime. Maybe I should just go back in time for school and settle."

Though Emma had been talking to herself more than Jules, he answered anyway. "You know, Emma, you don't have to go back home. You don't have to settle."

"I don't?" she asked, more confused than ever.

"No, you can stay here, with me."

Emma's mind stopped and she froze in his arms torn between her desire to go home, and her wish to stay here, in his arms, forever. She responded the only way she could think to. "Julian?"

"Yeah?"

"We're out of ice-cream."

26

Emma always thought it was weird how one minute you could be sitting there completely content with your life, and the next, questioning everything that you once wanted. She used to want to go to college at Dartmouth, get a degree in anything that sounded good on a resume, marry Luke, and plot out her life until retirement, but now, Emma discovered that the things that made her most happy were the very things that she knew had no future such as, sitting curled up in Julian's arms, or thinking about all of the things she could do with her life now that she had no ambitions, or expectations.

Maybe she'd travel the world.

Maybe she'd go skydiving.

Maybe she'd open a sanctuary for endangered monkeys in Singapore, or, probably not since she never cared for monkeys in the first place.

Maybe she'd stay with Julian forever.

Emma frowned. It didn't matter how many times she beat that thought out of her head, it kept forcing its way back in. She wanted him, craved him; hell, her body was on the point of near obsession with him, but if there was one thing she'd realized was true, it was that when Jules said that she'd never really loved Luke, he'd been right. Luke had hurt her, torn her heart apart in a way that made her think nothing in this world could mend it back together, even though Emma had never truly loved him. Thinking about how much she could be hurt by someone she only thought she had forced her to consider how much a person she truly loved could damage her fragile heart. The thought of that was too painful to bear.

Once again, Emma pushed the thought that said she could stay with Jules forever away. She'd put it tight inside a box with chains and throw it into an ocean, never to be seen again, though, it wasn't easy with Jules sitting there, being the most perfect man, as he had been the last two days.

It had been busy; Emma had moved her things into the house and set up her room, even though she had spent every night in Julian's. She'd also much of time dodging her father, Luke, and even Becca, whom she couldn't even consider facing. All of these exhausting activities preoccupied her mind, not allowing her to consider Jules' offer.

Jules had been even busier than she had. While he wanted nothing more than to spend all of the time that he could with Emma, now that he had finally broken her out of that angsty attitude; the fact that he released a new song, and the media had put him on high priority watch status, meant that he wasn't able to do everything he wanted, like make Emma so unendingly dizzy and distracted with kisses that she never remembered hating him.

Still, the two had fallen into a good rhythm; as long as Jules remembered not to remind her that she wasn't supposed to like him, then Emma felt just fine about giving her body what it wanted, which was more and more Julian.

"Remind me why I'm here again?" Emma whined.

"Because," Jules whispered to her, while steering her through the crowd with his hand on the small of her back. "I have to be here, which means that you have to be here."

"Why?" she asked again, resisting the urge to stamp her foot like a four year old.

Jules frowned, which was meant to hide his chuckle before saying, "Because the press needs to see how in love we are."

As he said it, Jules leant down to kiss Emma possessively on the mouth while the flashes around them went crazy. He stopped and turned to smile to the crowd, while Emma tried to regain her breath. She hoped that he didn't know that his touch still made her heart have little spasms in her chest.

They were at some unveiling of some new kind of technology which prevented music piracy or something or other; she hadn't been paying attention. Jules had been dressing when he'd told her, and his lean physique made it very hard to resist his request for her to accompany him.

Jules took her hand and led her to the bar to get a drink while being stopped half a dozen times along the way by preening fans or grasping celebrities.

Emma let her mind wander, which was something she should not have been doing. She had promised herself that she wouldn't think about the phone call she'd gotten that afternoon from her father, demanding that they have lunch tomorrow to "discuss things", but it couldn't be helped, she was nervous and Jules noticed, pulling her into a little, dark corner and looking at her with a serious expression on his face.

"What's wrong?" he asked.

"Nothing," Emma replied. "I'm just bored."

Jules snorted. "This is worse than just your normal hatred of doing these things with me. Now stop being a brat and tell me what's wrong."

Emma narrowed her eyes at him, but couldn't keep it up for long as he wound his fingers with hers.

"It's my dad. We're having lunch tomorrow."

He frowned for a second. "If you don't want to, then don't go."

"It's not that I don't want to its just—it's just, he's going to try and get me to leave."

Jules moved his hands up to cup her face. "Emma, you're not going anywhere."

She smiled at, about to say something, but Jules silenced her with a fierce kiss.

"Emma, please don't leave me," he said.

Emma looked at him and tried to keep the tears out of her eyes. His gray eyes glowed silver, like they did when he felt emotional.

At that moment, Emma knew what to say to him. "I'll never leave you."

27

"Sit down, Emma."

Her father's soft command did not go unnoticed as Emma sank into the soft, and comfortable, armchair at the small, but classy café her father had chosen to meet with her at. From the moment Emma walked in, she had been uneasy. Her father hadn't noticed her straight away, and in the second it took him to jump up from his chair, Emma had already spotted his drooped head and sagging shoulders. In all of her 18 years, she had only seen her father look that defeated once: the day her mother died. The thought had brought an unexpected rush of sympathy to her before turning to anger as she wondered whether that was his new tactic: use guilt to trick her into coming home with him.

Emma stiffened her shoulders and walked forward to meet him with the same determination to anger him as she had before she spotted his desolation. "Father."

A waiter arrived with a black coffee for her father and a ginger beer for her.

"I'm sorry," he said, "I ordered for you."

Emma frowned, she refused to admit to him that it was what she would have ordered for herself.

Her father sipped his coffee, studying her behavior.

Emma shifted under his gaze, her hands pulling on her black tights and plucking lint off the gray mini dress she wore. After another minute of his silent staring, and Emma's obvious avoidance of it, she looked at him and in a stern voice said, "So, I'm waiting. Aren't you going to start telling me how stupid I'm being and demand I come home with you?"

He just sighed, his bushy eyebrows bunching together. "You know," he said with a weight to his voice, different from the condemnation she had expected, "this morning when as I thought about this meeting, that was exactly what I planned to say to you. I planned to tell you that you were just a child, that you didn't know what you were doing—that there was nothing for you here."

Emma frowned and opened her mouth to speak, but he held up a hand.

"Please, let me finish. That was what I was going to say. But, on my way here from the hotel, I happened to spot this."

His wrinkled, heavy hand reached back into the coat hanging on the back of his chair and brought out a magazine. Her father handed it to her in silence, watching Emma's face as her eyes went to the picture of Jules, smiling a little to herself before turning to look at the less beautiful, but happy girl in his arms.

The title read "Jules And Emma In Love".

It was a picture from last night. *Man they got these things out quickly*, Emma thought. Jules held her face between his palms, and to the camera, it looked like they were about to kiss. Only Emma knew that it was actually the moment when she'd told Julian that she was never going to leave, and he had smiled at her with jovialness that it had frozen her for a second.

Emma swallowed the memory down hard so that she could look at her father stonily. "And what? You decided to bring this so that you could remind me that I was just a silly kid?"

Her father frowned again and something about it reminded Emma of sadness. "I brought that magazine, because when I looked at it, I realized...I realized that I have been blind and very wrong."

Emma blinked at him, not sure she comprehended what she had just heard.

"You love this boy."

Again, Emma just blinked.

"You love him, in a way that you never loved Luke. I can see that now. I can see that a part of you was just trying to please me with that relationship, even before you realized how much I had to gain from it."

Emma sensed shame in her father's voice.

She shook her head. "I don't understand, what—why are you saying this?"

"Because I love you, Emma, more than you think I do because of what I've done to you. I truly love you."

He bobbed his head slightly and took a sip from his coffee. Emma mimicked him and drank her ginger beer. It tasted bitter.

"When you said to me last week that I had tried to sell

you to Luke, I needed you to know that I never saw it that way. To my mind, as wrong and cruel as it turned out to be, to my mind, you and Luke were in love; so, when his parents offered me a way to repair what I had lost, it seemed the right—even the helpful thing to do."

A minute of silence followed before Emma said. "I don't think I ever really loved Luke."

To her surprise her father nodded. "I realized that this morning, when I saw this." He pointed to the magazine. "Up until then, all I'd know was that he loved you. I had no idea that you felt the same way."

"What would make you think we wouldn't love each other if we were engaged?"

"Emma, you and I both know that you hadn't met that boy until you ran away from Luke. I'm not blaming you, but I know you; you're far too guarded to let something like that genuinely happen."

Emma had to admit that that he was right. In general, aside from the Luke fiasco, she wasn't the kind of girl who just jumped into anything with reckless abandonment, particularly when she risked something as fragile as her heart.

Something else he'd said came back up, demanding her attention. "What did you mean when you said that you only knew that Jules loved me? He doesn't love me."

Her father smiled as though he recalled a fond memory. "Ahh, so you two have not got that far yet. Emma, for as little I can say that I know about Julian, I know that he loves you. That boy is infatuated."

Emma shook her head. "You can't know that, you've never even spoken to him."

Her father looked confused for a second, his brows crinkling. "Yes, I have. Last week at the hotel, when he came to pick up the rest of his things. After, the events, we talked, and while I was very determined to dislike the boy, I have to admit that he has a certain…integrity, which I respect."

Her father looked at her, expecting her to agree and start praising Julian.

Instead, Emma narrowed her eyes and asked, "What events?"

At this her father raised an eyebrow, wondering why she failed to understand him straight away. "I mean, when your "friend" Rebecca, once again, propositioned herself to Julian."

"Becca?" Emma blurted out, her voice dropping than a whisper. She felt like she'd just swallowed a block of ice; the cold swept over and encased her body until she felt the final plop as it landed in her gut.

"Yes, Becca. Of course, when I walked into his hotel room to, I'm sorry to say, try and scare him away from you, and saw him with the girl who was supposed to be your best friend I stormed off to tell you. I'm sorry to say that I was more than a little pleased to have my suspicions confirmed, but it seems that, that boy is as much a track star as a musician for how fast he caught up to me, and as much as I didn't want to believe that the affection, and attempt, was all on Becca's side, listening to Julian explain that he would never do anything to lose you—well, there is no doubting something when it is completely true."

The ice in Emma's stomach faded. While she was more revolted than she could possibly explain at the thought of

Jules' lips on Becca, a deep primal place in her recognized that he would never do that to her. Becca on the other hand—well, she was just a bitch! Emma couldn't wait to see those perky curls bounce when she punched Becca to the moon!

"Emma," her father said, "the real thing I wanted to say is that, I want you to be happy, and as much as I don't want to let you go, if being happy means you staying in London with Julian then I'm not going to stop you."

Emma blinked at him, certain that her hearing was faulty. She had no defense planned for compassion.

"I won't even disapprove, because I'll know that you'll be happy."

Emma's mind felt fuzzy, like someone scrunched tissue paper in her ear.

"Bu—but," she stammered, "what about Luke? What about the money you owe?"

"Let me worry about that, sweetheart, it was never your debt to repay, and your mother…your mother never would have wanted you to sacrifice anything. As for Luke, he is a complete and utter fool, and well, a bit of a prick. He'll back off once he knows there is no chance with you."

Emma still processed it; her father had given her permission to be with Julian. Without all of the drama, the hype, the lies, and the acting like she didn't feel for him the way she did.

She was still unmoving as she raised her voice just loud enough for her father to hear. "Dad," she began, while he leaned forward in his chair, "I want to go home."

28

Emma stood outside the house that had been her sanctuary, her paradise, the last few days; the one place on earth she felt was there solely for her happiness. She stood outside Jules' house and willed herself to say goodbye to it.

Sitting in the car with her father had been difficult. He didn't say much when she told him she wanted to go home. He asked her why, but Emma's only response was a shake of her head. "May be you should stay here," her father said when they pulled up in front of the house.

Emma stared at the building, its window flower beds and ornate shutters, and shook her head. She had to go, she had to get out, to get away before she was dragged in deeper, deeper than she could swim or fight to stay afloat. Falling in love with Jules wouldn't be lovely; it wouldn't be joyful, or like a pleasant glide through a cloudless sky. She would fall hard and fast and drown in her own unfathomable, unending love for him. It would consume her, and when he spat her back out, she would have nothing, and would feel like nothing.

Emma felt this love pulse within her chest as though it

were an entity with a will of its own as it rested next to her heart, which beat in hushed silence, a stark contrast to this new, more demanding life form. It terrified her.

Emma summoned her courage and got out of the car, walking up the narrow steps to the house, opened the door, and stepped inside. She moved as quietly as her feet allowed her to, hoping that Jules wasn't there to confront her, to stop her. The warmth inside the house melted some of her resolve.

She stopped in the doorway to his music room, which faced the garden, looking out at the courtyard where she'd once again let her passion get away from her. Jules sat on the piano stool, a guitar balanced in his arms as he strummed a muted melody. He didn't notice her at first.

As she studied him, Emma wondered why she hadn't realized that he possessed more than sexiness. He had a beauty, one for which was not visible on the outside, a kindness and gentleness, that Emma longed to be with, but was too frightened to admit it.

"Emma," Jules said, straightening when saw her. The smile that had been on his face faded the moment he saw her eyes. "Emma," he said again, his deep voice was grave now, "are you alright?"

Emma nodded.

Jules put the guitar down and walked to her, taking her hands, pulling her from the doorway and into the room. His arms circled around her, pushing her face into his chest. It was so natural, this little comfort, that Emma didn't jerk away from it.

"What happened?" He questioned, his voice still

strained. "Did your dad say something? Did he ask you to leave?"

Emma eased out of his arms, remembering what she was here to do.

"No," she replied, "he told me to stay. He said—he said he wants me to be happy."

Jules' brow furrowed for a moment as he tried to tie together this good news with the look of utter despair on Emma's face.

He looked at her, but she was glanced away, hiding her pale face with the thick curtain of her hair.

"Why do I get the feeling you're not happy?"

Emma bit her lower lip, unknowingly tempting Julian even then.

In a slow, and alien move, she wriggled out of his arms and, like always, they felt a little colder without her. "I'm leaving."

Her voice sounded stronger than she had expected it to, but Jules didn't believe her.

"What do you mean you're leaving?" he demanded.

"I'm going back home to be with my friends and family, and people who love me. It's where belong."

Jules raised an eyebrow, irritation nagged at him. Emma saw his confusion turn to resentment. *Maybe it was better this way*, she thought.

"I meant; what do you mean you're leaving when there is nothing for you back there?" Jules took a step towards her, bridging the space between them.

"That's not true!" Emma shot back. "I have plenty of things for me in America, like—"

"Family and friends, and people who love you," Jules finished for her, the sarcasm in his voice clear.

He took another step, his eyebrows lowering.

"What family? Your own father tried to sell you for Christ's sake!"

Emma opened her mouth to defend him but was cut of once again.

"Or maybe," Jules started, "you think Luke is your family; the same guy who was more than willing to drag you down the aisle rather than see you happy."

Emma looked at him, her eyes big as her bottom lip quivered. She'd never seen him like this. She had no idea that Jules, himself, was shocked by his own behavior, unsure of why his blood boiled. He knew that he should be gentle, trying to coerce her into staying, but he couldn't stand it. He didn't understand why, turning his confusion into anger, an anger that frightened Emma.

"But then," continued Jules "you could be going home for your friends, because really they all seem great. Your best friend came all the way to London, not to make sure you were safe, but to try and cheat with your boyfriend!"

Ignoring the sting of Becca's betrayal, Emma spat back, "I have other friends!"

"Of course you have other friends, but not ones who care enough to call you the entire time you were missing from the country!"

Emma didn't answer; she just stared at him. His eyes were silver again. She hated that she was doing this, that she angered him, and hated that what he said was correct. "What do you want me to say?"

Jules looked at her for a long moment, knowing that she wasn't this stupid, or this cowardly, to just give in and go home. He couldn't understand what she was running away from. "I want you to tell me the truth," he said, trying not to shout, "I want you to tell me why you're really leaving."

Emma's voice was still quiet, "I told you—"

"No!" Jules shot back. "That's not the reason you're going. Just tell me the truth, Emma! Why are you leaving? Why would—"

"Because I love you!"

Emma hadn't meant to say it; hadn't even known it was true until it burst from her mouth, but the moment it happened, she felt as though a giant weight had been taken off her chest. The thing next to her heart quivered with joy and she could no longer lie to herself about what she knew was true.

"I love you," she whispered.

Jules stood completely still; the only thing which showed any signs of life were his silver eyes which burned more than ever.

Suddenly, Emma's relief dissipated and her previous fears spewed to the top. "I love you and—and I'm scared! More scared than I've ever been in my life because I can't stop it! I can't not love you and—it kills me!"

She looked at him. She wanted to kiss him, like she always wanted to kiss him, but Emma couldn't move; she needed to hear him say it back. She needed it like her whole life rested on those words; she needed it, but waited, instead, for her heart to be broken.

Jules swallowed and his eyes asked the silent question of her leaving him.

"Just say that you love me," Emma pleaded. "Say you love me, and I'll stay. Nothing would take me away from you then. Just—just say that you love me, Julian."

They stood looking at each other, overwhelmed by what had happened as. Emma offered herself to him, more than her body, more than her surrender; she offered her soul to him, forever. All he had to do was say that he wanted her too.

Jules' fists clenched at his side and released as he opened his mouth to speak before closing it. Julian looked away, then back at her, before jerking away again, shaking his head.

Emma hadn't realized that she'd been holding one of her hands out to him, but she let it drop to her side. She looked at her hands hanging like dead weights as she stared at him in a daze. "You don't love me, do you?"

Emma looked up in time to see the edges of a frown and his one solemn nod. She remained frozen to the floor as the cool tracks of tears ran down her cheeks. "Goodbye, Julian."

Emma left, her deadened legs scraped through the hall until she reached the outside and ran.

She never stopped.

29

Sitting against the window in her home in New York, watching the snowflakes gather on the sills and wishing she had enough energy to get up and put on a sweater, Emma felt as though nothing had changed, while at the same time, everything had changed. She had visited her old friends, some of whom Emma knew hadn't even realized that she had been gone. She slept in her old bed, had gone to the deli that she used to love eating at, and nothing had changed.

But she had.

Sometimes Emma wondered if she would ever smile again. Sure she smiled at the easy routine that she had fallen back into, but there was always something unspoken behind it, some kind of effort that there hadn't been before. She found it difficult to be happy these days.

Sometimes, just when Emma thought she could move on, or forget, something would happen to bring her straight back to Jules, back to those days in London, which she dreaded revisiting because she knew that they would only make her see how hollow her life was.

Emma would see someone from behind who was tall, or broad shouldered, and her heart skipped a beat. When she walked in the park one day, a stranger smiled at her and Emma was reminded how inferior his smile was to Jules'.

It wasn't fair.

He was the one who didn't love her after all—it wasn't fair that, that little thing next to her heart was still there and beating strong, reminding her of her feelings for him. She shouldn't be the one having to suffer while he lived it up in London, going to parties and doing interviews with a new, and beautiful girl on his arm. Emma hadn't seen any of them, afraid that she might break down in tears, but it seemed like every time she looked at a magazine, or turned on the TV, there he was in all of his perfect glory put right in front of her just to torture her—to make it impossible to forget him.

So she didn't; she couldn't. He had been burned into her memory like a vicious type of static; you could try and drown it out, try and distract yourself from focusing on it, but it was always there, buzzing away in the background.

Emma pressed her face into the cold glass, watching the steam from her breath pool and contract. Her grief this time wasn't loud or resentful; it was a world away from what she'd felt about Luke. Instead of shouting to the world about her pain, she just wanted to disappear; she didn't want the pain to go because that would mean that Jules would go too, but she just—she just wanted it to stop.

While Emma wallowed in her grief, she remained un-aware that back in London, Jules suffered from heartache as well, wondering how could he have thought that one interview would make a difference. Jules walked through the snow, his publicist at his elbow, prattling on about damage control, but he didn't hear any of it. He tired of people talking to him. There was only one voice he wanted, and it was gone.

Jules ungloved hand reached up to rub the back of his neck as anger boiled beneath the surface, like he was trying to scratch away the skin.

His publicist slapped away his hand. "What have I told you about doing that?" she hissed.

His new habit was so frequent now that Jules didn't even notice it anymore; but other people did, and found the expression on his face when he rubbed at his skin a little too tormented to be marketable. *Well*, Jules thought, *they can go suck it!*

He didn't give a damn what they thought looked good or not, but still, he didn't say anything; he hadn't the energy to fight, or speak; he barely had the energy to breathe anymore for Christ's sake! Sometimes Jules thought he was being dramatic, but then he would remember something; like how she smelled of roasted coffee, even though she didn't drink it, or how he had never said things like "Christ's sake" before she came along, and he thought that nothing he did would be too dramatic.

For the first day or so, he hadn't realized that he missed her. He thought he had just felt guilty about the way things had ended between them, but when the ache refused to leave, kind of grew until it gnawed at him, Jules realized this wasn't normal. It was as though he had lost part of himself, and he almost felt like kicking his own arse for how long it took him to figure it out.

He loved her and he was the biggest jackass in the world.

He made her leave all because he couldn't pull his own head out of his ass long enough to realize what was right in front of him. Now, he could have shouted it to the sky that he loved her. HE LOVED HER!

As he reached up to rub at his jaw, Jules stopped himself halfway. "I have to do something," he said, more to himself than anyone else.

With that declaration, he spun around and got in the first taxi he saw.

30

Emma sat on her couch, a matted afghan cocooned around her, and about three days of left over makeup still on her face when her father walked in. Things had been improved between them. After leaving London, he had obeyed her no speaking, referring, or alluding to anything to do with Julian decree. He even brought Emma the essentials for the silent pity parties she held in her room every night: Krispy Kreme doughnuts and a never ending supply of kids movies, which Emma had found were the only movies that were entertaining without focusing on love. She had been in Richie Rich heaven for the past week.

The real bonding moment, which had made Emma truly forgive her father, happened when Luke had managed to force his way inside to see her. It had not been pretty. Luke's version of a tantrum made a nuclear warhead look like a fire cracker, but amid Luke's demanding, bragging, and gloating over Emma and Jules' breakup, something truly amazing had happened: her father had looked at Emma's tearful eyes, walked across the room, and punched Luke in the face.

While the punch of a 55 year old man was only enough to make Luke stumble a little, it had the benefit of waking Emma up, bringing her back to life, enough for her to storm across the room and punch Luke herself. Not only did he fall, he crashed into the coffee table.

Though the relationship between her and her father was back on track, Emma was too much of an emotional zombie to even be happy about it. In fact, if she really had become a zombie it wouldn't surprise her. At least, it would explain why, when he walked in, it took Emma about three minutes to realize he was even there, standing over her.

"Um, sorry, what did you say?" she asked, trying not to sound like the undead.

Her father sighed but tried to hide it. "I asked what you were doing."

Emma looked around for something to distract her from what she had really doing, slowly becoming comatose, and settled on the shiny screen in front of her. "I was just about to watch some TV." she said with a smile, picking up the remote and flicking it on.

Her eyes only had time to focus for a second on the gorgeous, gleefully smiling face which already haunted her before she slammed the off button. Recovering quickly, Emma pulled the blanket off herself and stood up. "Actually, I think I'll just go have a nap."

Emma had little time to feel the new wave of despair wash over her before her father barked her name; followed by a rare demand.

"Come back here."

Emma went to him, her eyes downcast, hating for him

to see the pain consuming her. To her surprise he didn't try to talk to her; he just grabbed her shoulders and pushed her down so she sat on the couch. Her father reached around her, rewrapping the blanket tightly, so her whole upper body was bound, and with one hand he held the ends.

"What are you doing?" Emma demanded, so dumbfounded that she forgot her pain for a moment.

"Keeping you still," her father replied.

"Why?"

"Because," he said, picking up the remote, "I'm not letting you run away anymore."

He turned the TV on.

Emma flinched away from the screen, averting her face, while trying to get up, but the blanket held her firm. She caught a glimpse of a gray eye and jerked wildly. "Turn it off!" Emma shouted. "I don't want to watch."

"Amanda," her father said, "watch the screen."

Emma turned her face, choking back a sob as Julian's entire god-like figure filled the screen.

He sat on a red couch; his legs slightly spread apart, a hand resting on each knee, and just as he shook his head to whatever question he was just asked, Emma realized that he looked more tense than she'd ever seen him in any interview. Julian opened his mouth and from the first words Emma was fixed; she couldn't have moved now if she wanted to. She was hypnotized. She wanted to press her face to the screen.

The camera flicked over to the host and Emma recognized him as British. It took a minute for the buzzing in Emma's head to clear before she actually heard their conversation.

"Julian. Julian, it's like you were designed to make the rest of us look bad," said the host.

Jules smiled and shook his head.

"No, come on," the host persisted, "not only have you had an absolute orgy of hits yourself, which are, I'm the first to admit, surprisingly not horrendous, but now, your record label Playground is responsible for some of the finest musicians around. You've got to be a little impressed with yourself."

Jules bit his lip and Emma groaned into her mouth.

"I'm absolutely thrilled and so proud of the artists that Playground are releasing at the moment. They are all so amazing and somehow, completely one of a kind, each of them. So, yeah, I'm proud as punch of Playground, but I'm, definitely not impressed with myself," Jules finished with a little grin which tried, but didn't quite soften the words.

"Oh come on, don't go emo on me now, Julian."

He laughed, but like Emma's, there was an edge to it now.

"Oh, shoot me if I become emo, Dave. I guess I just meant, I can't see a reason to be proud of myself at the moment."

The host's eyes widened like he'd just struck gold.

"Really? And why is that, Julian?"

Emma saw his hand stretch up and scratch at the side of his face. She wanted to grab it and make him stop.

"I—I was stupid. I did something stupid. I suppose

that maybe I always was just this stupid, little prick who never thought about anything other than myself; but it took losing something, someone, for me to realize it."

The host's eyes popped out of his skull for one second before he nodded and went into journalist mode. "Am I right in assuming, then, that this someone could be Emma Corzeica?"

Jules didn't answer; he just smiled in that sad way and scratched his jaw again.

Emma watched as the host's eyes darkened into something more genuine. "Being in love is the worst wake-up call of all."

Julian's grin was genuine this time. "You've got that right."

Emma didn't even notice that the blanket had gone slack around her. She couldn't have moved even if she wanted to.

"And I believe that you are going to make all the ladies in the world fall even more in love with you now by singing us a song?"

Jules looked relieved that the host had lightened the tone. "Yeah, that's right. This is a new one too, never been heard before."

"A world first!"

Jules smiled and picked up an acoustic guitar. His husky voice in the microphone sent a shiver through Emma. "This is called *Ten Days*."

Jules started humming quietly alone with the melody, as though urging himself to sing.

So we've put an end to it this time.
I'm no longer yours and you're no longer mine.
You said this hill looks far too steep
But I'm sure that its you, I wanna keep.
And it's been ten days without you in my reach,
And the only time I've touched you is in my sleep.

But time has changed nothing at all.
You're still the only one that feels like home.
I've tried cutting the ropes and
I let you go; but you're still the only one
That feels like hope.

You won't talk me into it next time,
If I'm going away your hearts coming too.
Cuz, I miss your hands; I miss your face.
When we get back let's disappear without a trace.

Cuz, its been ten days without you in my reach,
And the only time I've touched you is in my sleep.

But time has changed nothing at all.
You're still the only one that feels like home.
I've tried cutting the ropes,
Tried letting go, but you're still the only one
That feels like hope.

So tell me, did you really think...
Oh tell me, did you really think
I had gone, when you couldn't see me anymore?

When you couldn't...

Cuz, baby, time has changed nothing at all
You're still the only one that feels like home.
And I've tried cutting the ropes.
I let you go; but you're still the only one
That feels like hope, yeah,
You're still the only one that feels like hope,
You're still the only one I've gonna love.
Oh yeah...
You're still the only one I'll ever love...

The last notes were followed by a banging applause from the live audience, but everything was muffled to Emma.

Tears streamed down her cheeks, but she never wiped them away, and her father had long since left the couch, but she wouldn't have known.

He loved her .He loved her .He loved her, and because she'd been acting like such a self-centered, emotional wreck, she hadn't known it until now. Emma would have kicked herself if she hadn't thought that would only waste more time.

Somehow, in her hysteria, Emma managed to grab her passport and a credit card, but other than that, everything was a maddening blur until she leapt out of the still moving cab at the airport. Emma thought that there would never be a more welcome sight than the departure gate that she threw herself towards. Stuck in a horde of fat vacationers, making their slow way back from their Christmas holidays,

Emma felt as though she was drowning in a sea of smiling, pointless faces as they ambled along.

She stopped, her passport and boarding pass hanging by her side as she recognized one face in particular.

Emma had always thought that it was ridiculous when people described those moments that made time still, but at that moment, she thought that there was nothing moving, nothing breathing, but their two faces in the crowd. Just midnight and gray eyes captivated by a single moment, a moment none, but them, would understand.

While Emma looked at Jules' perfect face and froze, he stared at her and took one, very deep breath before throwing his bag to the ground and sweeping her into his comforting arms.

31

There were many things that Jules had planned to say when he saw Emma again: that he loved her; that he was a douchebag, and that it didn't matter what he did because he was never going to be able to forget her. But when he saw her standing in the airport, wedged between scrambling tourists, her eyes wide like she'd just woken up from a nightmare, all the careful speeches that Jules had prepared earlier escaped him. There was nothing more natural, or essential, than swinging her up into his arms and kissing her.

His lips closed around her soft ones, which quivered before sinking into his. Emma's hands went clutched the shoulders of his jacket, his neck, anything, to pull him closer and support her as she wrapped her legs around his waist.

Jules rejoiced. He felt alive again. Alive and in the arms of the person he loved more than anything he could imagine. more than any fantasy girl he could make up. Jules honestly didn't think they would ever stop kissing. Why would they? What else would they possibly need than this? So, it was a shock to him when he was broken from his haze by the sound of flashes going off around them.

Reluctantly, he broke his lips from hers and looked around them. A small, but rapidly growing crowd had gathered, pulling out disposable cameras and cell phones to record the sudden celebrity peep show that had popped up in front of them. He looked back at Emma, whose legs were still wrapped around his middle, her hands buried in his hair. She was bit her lip and her deep blue eyes widened at him as though she couldn't believe what she'd just done.

It occurred to Jules, at that moment, that he might not be forgiven for hurting her. Maybe she still didn't know.

Emma's hands slid down to his shoulders where they tightened as she unwrapped herself from him. She looked to the crowd around them and then past the sea of jumping, gawking expressions, looking for an exit.

Jules saw her looking and resisted the urge to throw her over his shoulder and walk off with her. Instead he just grabbed her hand and pulled her through the nearest door.

Emma looked around her. *A bathroom?*

Jules had taken her, for their grand reunion, for the conversation which would decide their future happiness, to the men's room at the JKF airport. She wondered how they could confess their love amid the sting of toilette paper strewn across the tile floor and mildew stained sinks that threatened to have something unsavory crawl out of it. Emma touched her lips. They had kissed, they had kissed and it had been…it had been like they were both in love.

A flush rang around them before a red faced man in tweed threw open a stall door. He looked at Emma, then behind him, then to Emma again, before dropping his jaw and looking at Jules, who opened the door to the exit before saying in a harsh voice, "Out, please."

The man furrowed his brows, but finished buttoning his trousers before rushing out the door. Emma couldn't help but notice that he didn't wash his hands. *How gross!*

Emma didn't want to turn around, didn't want to face him. That kiss haunted her; too beautiful, too perfect to not be followed by something that was sure to break her heart, again, but when she heard the scraping of metal, the confusion forced her to spin on her heels just in time to see Jules dragging the metal trash can under the door handle. Emma understood the logic; she didn't want any more people bursting in to take a friendly pee in the urinal.

Jules looked at her with nervous apprehension and gave her a half smile. Emma's heart clenched. *Oh god! Why did he have to be so flipping gorgeous?* she thought to herself.

"Emma," he said and took a step towards her. He stopped and shook his head like he was trying to find the right words. "Emma, I..." He stopped again and reached his hand up to grate at his jaw.

"Stop that!" Emma demanded, reaching forward and yanking his hand away. To her disbelief, Jules chuckled.

"You know you're about the 80th person to do that to me."

Emma raised an eyebrow at him and bit her lip before smoothing her fingers over the raw skin.

He closed his eyes.

"Just stop." She said.

Jules nodded, his eyes opening to the silver which had followed Emma everywhere.

His hands looped around at her waist and Emma's hand stayed pressed to his face.

"I saw the interview," she said. "I'm sorry it took me so long."

Jules shook his head. "I'm sorry that I thought it would be enough."

Emma wanted to tell him that it was enough; that the song, and the way he spoke, had proved it to her, but she wasn't sure. She swallowed. "What are you doing here?"

Jules looked down at her and wished that he could take off his jacket so that they could be closer. "I—I had to see you. I had to tell you everything that was wrong with me, with what I had said. I had a speech planned and everything."

Emma frowned. "I was coming to see you, you know. I saw the interview today—my dad made me watch it—and I just, sprinted out of the house."

Emma moved her hand down to his arm; she needed to ask, she had to know, but she was too proud to voice the question on her mind; and last time, when he hadn't said it back, it had broken her. She looked down, away from him. Emma didn't know if she could survive such misery again.

Jules' fingers found her chin and tilted it up to him. He sucked in a quick breath. She was so beautiful; her dark eyes shining, her hair in a knotted pony tail on top of her head, and her little pointed chin quivering. He didn't want to hold it in anymore; he didn't want to wait. "I love you, Emma."

Her eyes widened and her mouth opened, then closed again.

His fingers stroked her cheeks, running over the smooth skin of her lips. "I love you, and I'm not just saying that because I missed you, or because standing here you're the most beautiful thing I've ever seen. I'm telling you, because I love you, because, without you, my world was so gray— that there was no point to it at all."

Emma looked at him anew as his words washed over her like the brightest happiness she could imagine.

"And I could kick myself a million times for not saying it back to you. I'll regret that forever."

Emma started to speak but he pressed his fingers to her lips.

"I never really thought that I deserved your love, because you have every kind of strength that I wanted, but, Emma, I do love you so much."

She moved her hands to his chest.

"I want to be with you forever and if that means waiting 20 years to get married, when all the money is gone, I will. Just so you can know that I want you for you, and that I'll want you forever."

Emma stood on her tiptoes, and slowly, carefully, pressed her lips to his: it was a kiss and an answer. "I love you, Jules."

He smiled then, and Emma's heart flipped over in her chest.

"Just one thing," Emma said.

"What?" Jules asked, wrapping his arms around her.

"Did you have to tell me that in the bathroom?"

32

Two months later...

Emma smiled as she ripped open the top of the care-package her father had sent her, giggling to herself: another scarf. Her father had sent her twelve since Emma had moved to London.

At first, she had complained about it; but now welcomed the scarfs, having to wear three every time she stepped out of the apartment. Though, Emma kind of liked the cold now.

The cold meant heaps of good things: fireplaces, big jackets, being able to drink hot chocolate without everyone thinking you were eight, and cuddles: Emma couldn't forget all the cold days spent snuggling with Jules.

Emma dug further into the package and brought out a beautiful pen engraved with her initials and a notepad. She smiled when she opened the notepad to find that someone had already drawn math timetables into the front. Emma was touched by her father's gesture, but she thought that because she was going to be studying music production and publishing, she wouldn't need math. At least, she hoped not.

Emma's acceptance letter to Oxford had come last week. It turned out that before she had fled back to the States, Jules had already sent in an application form for her. At first Emma was mildly pissed that he'd done it behind her back, but after realizing that she might have the chance to go to one of the best schools in the world, she shut her mouth, went to an interview and—voila!—She was officially a university student.

As for what she wished to study, that was a much easier decision than she ever could have guessed. After following Julian to his studio for about three weeks straight as he recorded a new album, she realized that she had a flair for production and promotion. Jules had said she was so good at it because she was naturally dramatic. Emma had just slapped him on the back of the head and told him not to mock her talent.

She looked across the kitchen table at Jules. He read the paper, his dark hair messy from bed, while simultaneously lifting his cereal bowl to his lips to drink the milk. Jules liked Fruit Loops.

That was just one of the surprising things Emma had discovered about him, but after living with him, she found out a lot more: Jules didn't know how to wash his clothes. He liked to hand wash the dishes, even though he had a dishwasher, and if Emma let him; he would sleep on top of her every night. For some reason, though, it worked. She taught him how to use the washing machine, and he taught her how to enjoy washing up the dishes; a lesson mostly ended in a sudsy water fight: and, secretly, Emma loved Fruit Loops, almost as much as she loved it when Jules rolled over to her in the middle of the night and threw himself on top of her. Even if she could barely breath, she was home. Emma never slept better.

She loved getting these packages and letters from her father. At first they'd always contained some piece of gossip, like how Emma's friends from school wouldn't stop coming around to the house since they found out she was dating Jules. Or talking about how, thanks to the modest loan Julian, had given her father, he had paid of his debts and was rebuilding his company, doing better than even Emma could have hoped for.

The most shocking bit of news came about a month after Emma had moved to London with Jules. Her father had written this letter to Julian, not her, thinking that if she was upset it might be better to hear it from him. She remembered Jules' had look of concern when he told her that Luke and Becca had just been married.

Emma didn't understand, she wasn't upset, just confused. When she asked why, her father had written that Luke's family had found out that Becca was pregnant: three months pregnant, with Luke's baby. As quickly as Emma had realized that this meant they'd been sleeping together while she was engaged to him, she burst out laughing. They were both horrible people, but even Emma thought that having to spend their lives together was a bit of a harsh punishment.

She hadn't really thought about it much after that. It didn't matter. She was happy.

It didn't matter to her when things weren"t perfect, or when Emma made a fool of herself, because Jules loved her for that. He loved her for her clumsiness, or the fact that she was as likely to kick him as to kiss him. And Emma knew: she didn't even need to hear him say it anymore to know that it was true.

When they would walked down the street and Emma would spot girls looking at him like they'd sell their souls to touch him, she would just smile and keep walking. Let them have their fantasies: he was all hers.

Even when a particularly eager teen managed to scrambled over the barricades at some party they were at last week and kiss him full on the mouth, Emma hadn't flinched. She just watched as Jules extracted himself and sent her on her way, with Emma only giving the girl one, little kick in the shins for good measure.

Jules looked at her from across the table, milk dripping from his chin. "What are you smiling at?" he asked, suspicion filled his voice.

"Memories."

Jules raised an eyebrow, but turned his head back to the paper, before grabbing one of her hands and playing with her fingers.

Emma smiled. It was simple: they were in love and the world felt brighter. Emma spent her time surrounded by thunderstorms and peppermint, silver and bed hair, and she loved it. Reaching back into the package, she pulled out the last thing her father had sent: a magazine.

Emma had seen so many magazines lately, ranging from the ridiculous to the grotesquely soppy, that she'd stopped looking at them. This one had another picture of them on the front. They were just walking down the street, only their hands touching. The beautiful rock star and the slightly less beautiful, but glowing, girl beside him.

Emma's eyes moved to the heading. "Emma and Jules Live Happily Ever After," she read aloud.

"Wow," said Julian, resting his chin on her shoulder, "they finally got one right."

"Yeah," Emma smiled, turning to face him, "they really did, didn't they."

About the Author

Brie Kraus always dreamed of being a writer, but put that ambition on hold, while pursuing working in the fast food industry and putting herself through college. After graduating and losing her employment, Ms. Kraus turned back to her forgotten dream: writing. Don't' Ask is her first novel, closely followed by I Hate Your Rock Stars. She has also written a mystery, short read series (Closed Case).

More By Brie Kraus